The Mc

(The Aftermath of ꟷoor.
The last battle ꟷsoil)

A Novel

by

Suzanne David

BARHAM MANOR, BRIDGWATER
22ND JUNE 1685

SARAH COULDN'T SLEEP, her husband William was snoring. It had never occurred to her that she would miss the irritating sound. She was fearful that it was a noise she would never hear again.

She pushed herself up on to her elbow and studied him in the moonlight as he slept. William Barham was 36 years old, a tall man, broad shouldered and muscular. His once luxurious chestnut brown hair was thinning. Sarah touched it gently and sighed, she loved him so much.

William had served as a captain in the Royal English Regiment during the Anglo-Dutch War under the command of the Duke of Monmouth. Injury to his right arm had caused William to be invalided out of the regiment. Sarah hoped and prayed that her husband would use his disability as a reason to stay away from trouble, but she feared he couldn't wait to be in Monmouth's service once more. Sarah lay down again and tried to sleep.

***

THE PREVIOUS DAY Bridgwater had been in uproar. The exhilarating sound of drums had announced the arrival of the rebel army of James Scott, Duke of Monmouth. There had been pandemonium and disorder everywhere. Dogs barking, children animated, men excited and women frightened, alarmed by the chaos that the arrival of the Duke had caused.

A civic reception had been hastily arranged and William had been part of the welcoming committee during which the Duke of Monmouth had been crowned king by the mayor of Bridgwater. It was Monmouth's third coronation; he had also been crowned in Chard and Taunton.

In the evening, Sarah's family had sat in their garden after supper. The warm summer night had made seven-year-old Harry sleepy, but ten-year-old Paul had been animated.

"Father, at school all the older boys were talking about the Duke of Monmouth. I don't understand how he can be crowned king when we already have King James."

"I was going to talk to you about what happened today Paul, Harry are you listening as well?"

Harry sat upright "Yes father."

"James, Duke of Monmouth claims he is the legitimate son of Charles II. He had been groomed by his father to expect to inherit the throne when he died. The Duke was in Holland in the service of William, Prince of Orange when his father passed away. In his absence James, Duke of York the Catholic brother of King Charles claimed the throne."

The children's pretty kitten suddenly decided at that moment to jump on William's lap, he pushed her off roughly.

"Get off me Polly!"

"William!"

"Father!" Three pairs of angry eyes were looking at him.

"Her paws are dirty, look at my trousers!" William was hurt by the lack of sympathy.

"Polly, come here Polly." Paul gathered up the frightened kitten. "You can sit on my lap."

"I'm sorry I didn't mean to frighten her, now where was I?"

"You had explained that the Duke of York had claimed the throne."

"Well done, Harry, you have been listening." William looked surprised. "Paul, I saw that!" He had seen Paul sticking his tongue out at his brother. "I will continue now that the cat is comfortable. Monmouth, a Protestant, initially went into hiding in Holland but eventually decided to claim the throne he had been brought up to believe was his. He landed a few weeks ago in Lyme Regis in Dorset, where he was welcomed by 3,000 men."

"The boys at school said their fathers are going to join him."

"Are you going to join him father?" Said Harry excitedly.

Sarah gave her husband a worried look. The subject was the cause of many arguments between them.

"Harry let me continue please. The 3,000 men who met Monmouth at Lyme Regis marched with him to Chard then on to Taunton. In addition to these men, Monmouth has an ally – the Duke of Argyle who has started a rebellion in Scotland."

Little Harry interrupted, he was slow to keep up and he was puzzled. "So, we have two kings?"

"Only King James has been officially crowned Harry, but many people do not want Catholic King James to be their king."

"Do we now call the Duke of Monmouth King James as well?"

"We can't really, can we? It would be too confusing." William smiled at his son.

Sarah was on her feet. "I thought that was rain I felt. Boys, William, help me get the washing in. By the time the servants realise it's raining it will be too late. Quickly!" Sarah ran across the garden as a flash of lightening illuminated the sky.

That night in bed Sarah again broached the vexed subject of William joining Monmouth. The answer was still the one she did not want to hear.

As she tossed and turned, Sarah recalled her parents taking her to see her three-year-old cousin die. She had been upset by the experience. Trying to comfort her later her mother had explained that it was part of the *'preparation for death'* a religious process to help Christians reach a state of peaceful acceptance. Sarah understood that her parents had meant well but knew she wouldn't have peaceful acceptance if William died.

***

"YOU NEED TO tell the boys." Sarah was tight lipped; she had dark circles under her eyes from crying.

"Send them to me." Sarah rang the bell for the housemaid. "Jessie, please can you ask masters Paul and Harry to join us." She turned to William, "I am afraid. The boys will be excited, they will see it as a great adventure. They won't understand the danger. William, if you join Monmouth you will be branded a traitor, you a man who held the King's commission!"

"We are a Protestant family. It is my duty to help Monmouth, a Protestant, become king." Paul and Harry had entered the room. "Boys did you both eat your breakfast?"

"Yes father. Mabel made us special oatmeal." Harry's little face was flushed from too much to eat.

"And what may I ask is special oatmeal?"

"It has stewed apples mixed in with it and then cream on top."

"Well, I must say that is a good way to start the day. I will ask Mabel for special oatmeal for my breakfast tomorrow. Now, I have something of importance I must tell you both."

"You look serious father." Paul looked from his father to his mother. "Mother looks upset."

"Boys, I will be joining the Duke of Monmouth's army. That means I will march with him. I don't know how long I will be away. Paul, you will be the man of the house and must look after your mother. Harry, you must be a good boy and not cause either your mother or your brother any trouble. Do you understand?"

"Yes father". Both boys looked serious.

TWO DAYS LATER

"SARAH, TELL THE servants we will be receiving a guest. The Duke of Monmouth will be dining with us. We need the best china, our finest wine, a splendid menu, we need to speak to Mabel." William was animated.

"Its such short notice." Sarah was ringing the bell to summon the cook.

"Sir, madam, is everything alright?" Mabel arrived looking worried. William never interfered in the workings of her kitchen.

"Mabel, our house is being honoured by the presence of the Duke of Monmouth. He will be joining us for dinner tonight. Mabel.... Sarah quick, a seat." Mabel swayed, her face ashen. William quickly picked up the pitcher of water and filled a glass. He handed it to Mabel.

"I'm so sorry sir, madam. I don't know what came over me. I can't take it in, the Duke of Monmouth eating my food! I'm not up to it."

"Yes, you are, you are the finest cook in Bridgwater," said Sarah. "Don't be falsely modest Mabel. Pull yourself together and let us work out a menu."

As the day wore on the entire household was in a state of feverish fear and excitement. Fear that they could not reach the standards required to entertain a duke and excitement at the thought of being part of such a remarkable occasion. Paul and Harry couldn't wait to tell their friends. All the servants were relishing the thought of their status in the town when it was known that they worked in the house where the Duke of Monmouth had dined.

Dear Pam,

I hope you

enjoy it.

Suzanne

x x

AS SHE WAITED impatiently for her maid to finish dressing her hair Sarah remembered many years earlier when she was a small child standing at the door of her mother's bedroom. She had watched fascinated as her mother's maid had prepared her mistress to meet the young Charles II. All the best families of Bridgwater had been invited to the castle to meet their king.

Sarah studied herself in the mirror. Her golden-blond hair was being expertly styled. She was pretty, and she knew it. Her heart-shaped face and large violet eyes had attracted many suitors. She smiled, none as handsome as William she thought.

The evening was a success. Mabel had drummed up extra help in the kitchen, the butcher had supplied the very best meat. William's uncle, who had founded the family's shipping business, had stocked the cellar with some superb wine. The red from Bordeaux had been particularly appreciated by the Duke.

Monmouth was so pleased with the meal that he asked to complement the cook. A nervous Mabel had entered the dining room and had nearly fallen when she attempted a deep curtsy. She was almost overwhelmed when Monmouth helped her to her feet. Mabel stuttered her appreciation of the thanks she received and retreated hastily from the dining room.

Her son Ben, who had been hauled in as extra help in the kitchen was nearly knocked over by his mother when she triumphantly burst through the kitchen door.

"The Duke said he thought the meal was excellent." She cried. Ben led her to a chair and handed her a large glass of ale, which she raised in praise of her staff.

"I wouldn't have managed it without you all. Remember this day, we may not all be marching but we have sent the Duke on his way with a contented belly."

After the meal, the evening was still warm enough for William and the Duke to take their wine out into the garden. Monmouth strolled across the lawn to the bank of the river Parrett.

"My plan is to march to Bristol and then on to London." He turned, "Your wife Sarah is the most delightful woman and a charming hostess; however, I sense that she quite naturally is concerned about you marching with me."

"All the wives are concerned sir; it is to be expected. Sarah is a soldier's daughter. She knows I must do my duty and she will support me. We both believe in the Protestant cause."

***

THE NEXT MORNING Monmouth led his 7,000 strong army out of Bridgwater and on through Westonzoyland, Glastonbury and Pensford. They met up with the King's army near Keynsham where they suffered heavy losses. There was another skirmish at Norton St Philip where they successfully ambushed the King's army.

They marched on to Frome, where the weather turned against them. The inclement weather, combined with the defeat at Keynsham caused many men to drift off home, disillusioned and demoralised. The disturbing news that the Duke of Argyle had been defeated in Scotland meant that the success of the Protestant cause now depended solely on Monmouth. He knew he needed a quick victory against the royalist army before any more of his men drifted away.

A depleted army of 3,500 men returned to Bridgwater on 2 July, brave men but inexperienced and poorly armed. There was none of the wild enthusiasm that had greeted Monmouth 12 days earlier. An air of failure hung around the weary soldiers. The women of the town prepared hot food and tended to wounds where needed.

Some of the Bridgwater men knew which doors to knock on if a man felt in need of a woman and passed the information on to their new comrades. The town, so silent after the men marched out was buzzing with activity.

Sarah, Paul and Harry were overjoyed to have William back home. After the initial exuberant welcome, Sarah's mood changed when she realised that William intended to march on with Monmouth.

"Sarah, there have been Bridgwater men killed, many injured. I owe it to them to continue. I cannot let their deaths be in vain." Sarah knew there was no point in arguing.

***

ON 5 JULY MONMOUTH received the news that the Royalist army was camped in Westonzoyland, five miles from Bridgwater. At William's suggestion, Monmouth had accompanied him up the tower of St. Mary's church and, using an eyeglass, Monmouth could see the Royalist encampment.

At 11 o'clock that evening Monmouth led his men out of Bridgwater and along the Bristol Road. They were a troop of countrymen, farmers and tradesmen unskilled in the art of war marching steadfastly towards an army of trained soldiers. Monmouth, encouraged by the report that many of the King's troop had been drinking, felt more positive about the battle than he had the day before. His newfound confidence was tempered by his knowledge of the men of the King's army, men he had served with in the past. He knew that their experience made them dangerous even if they were hungover.

Monmouth's volunteer army managed to get close to the royal encampment and he was pleased as it appeared they would have the advantage of a surprise attack, but it was not to be. An accidental musket shot by one of his men raised the alarm. His cavalry made a courageous charge but were cut down by the Royalist guns. Panic spread amongst his untrained troops and many were slaughtered. The day was lost. Within hours 22 rebels had been hanged, 500 rebels were locked up in West-onzoyland church, and a further 19 hanged the next day.

William had been captured. He was in the church. He had often worshiped in St. Mary the Virgin. He and Sarah had attended the wedding of one of Sarah's cousins there. Now he was squashed up against a wall, surrounded by bloody, sweating men. There were terrible sounds; some of the imprisoned men were in agony. The defeated rebels awaited their fate. Monmouth had gone.

FOUR HOURS LATER

"DO YOU HAVE any idea at all as to how many prisoners we are holding here?" A tall man in an officer's uniform had entered the church. William was jolted out of his reverie. He recognised the officer's voice, the educated tones so different from the West County burr humming around him. William stopped slouching against the wall and stood up straight. He could now see the familiar face of his brother-in-law. His heart was beating heavily in his chest. Should he make himself known? Before he had time to come to a conclusion, Captain Clive Pemberton-Harvey had spotted him.

"Sergeant, I need to speak to that man over there in private. It is possible that he can be of assistance in helping us find Monmouth. I will wait for him in the church yard. Bring him to me." The soldier saluted and pushed his way through the throng of prisoners, making his way slowly towards William.

"This way, follow me." The soldier pushed William ahead of

him, and they slowly made their way outside. The sun was setting, the gloomy sky making the spectacle of bodies handing from trees even more horrific than it had been in bright sunlight. William recoiled at the sight. He felt sick.

"Prisoner take a seat. That will be all sergeant."

William was glad to sit. He felt weak and shocked at the cruelty of the King's army. Clive waited until the soldier had left.

"I am dismayed to find you here. Whatever were you thinking man? Sarah. The boys!"

"I joined Monmouth because I saw my clear duty was to support him. His father expected him to be king. Monmouth is a good Protestant. A good man, you of all people should understand my allegiance to him after I served with him in Holland. You were there, you know the loyalty Monmouth had towards his men."

"Time is short, maybe one day we can debate where your allegiance should lie. Just now I must avoid the disgrace that will come to my family if my brother-in-law is hung for treason." William said nothing, just stared at the bodies of his former comrades swaying slowly in the wind. He felt tears coming to his eyes as one of the bodies swung around and he could see the face of the victim. It was Tom Colford; he had left a wife and five children. William knew there was another child on the way.

"William, for God's sake man, listen to me! I will help you." William forced himself to concentrate on his own problem.

"If you help me then you must help two more people."

"What! I don't believe this! You are in no position to ask a favour."

"Your sergeant in Holland – Reginald Turle. His sons are in the church."

"My God, how could you have allowed them to get mixed up in

this mess. They are boys not men. If Sergeant Turle had still been alive, he would never have allowed it."

"Well he isn't, and you know why. If it weren't for him, you would not be here today. You owe it to his memory. And you owe it to his widow. She cannot survive without her boys. She bought a small farm with Turle's pension, she can't work it on her own."

"Sergeant – over here. Quickly man." The sergeant who had bought William out of the church was leaning against a tree smoking.

"You must find – what are their names?"

"Thomas and Matthew Turle." William had stood up. He was feeling more positive about life.

"Sergeant you heard that. Find them and bring them to me." As soon as the sergeant was out of earshot Clive turned to William. "You are beholden to me. Someday I will come to you for help and you must honour your debt to me." Clive held out his hand. William took it.

"Understood."

"I will arrange horses for you. You must get away from the battlefield. You have money I presume." William nodded. "You must lie low. You should not return to Bridgwater for at least two weeks, and then you will be wise to approach the town with caution. Do not get caught. Remember, I am only helping you because I am married to your wife's sister. Do not bring shame on her and my nephews."

"I can assure you Clive that I will do my very best to avoid the noose." William had never been comfortable in the company of Clive but had always been cordial towards him for Sarah's sake. Now he wished he had the freedom to punch Clive on the nose but knew that would be suicidal.

***

IN THE MEANTIME, the women of Bridgwater had all gathered in St. Mary's Church. They had even been joined by some women from Taunton who had ridden the nine miles between the towns, desperate for news of their menfolk.

The vicar, the Reverend Hugh Staunton offered comfort where he could. The church was quiet. Some women were whispering to each other, some sat with their eyes closed, silently mouthing their prayers. Occasionally the crying of a baby shattered the stillness. The vicar's wife and daughters had rounded up the older children and taken them to play in the ruins of the castle, away from the distress of their mothers. Suddenly the peace was shattered by the arrival of a horseman. He burst through the door, dishevelled and blood splattered.

"Disaster, we have lost! Our men cruelly treated. They have hung many!" The messenger collapsed, his knees giving way, his grief too much for him to bear. There was silence, then sobbing, then a surge of activity. The vicar assisted the man to a chair.

"Can someone go quickly to the vicarage. The door is open, find some ale and bring it to me. This man is in need of sustenance."

"Where are the survivors?"

"Are many wounded?"

"Is there anything we can do; do you know who has died?" The distraught women clamoured for more information.

A girl arrived with a flask of ale, the messenger drank the liquid, his thirst obvious to those watching him. "We thought we could surprise 'um; but it all went wrong. They have locked our men in Westonzoyland church. Hung others – hanging from the trees everywhere - a terrible sight."

There was a commotion at the door. Several more men, dishevelled and bloody staggered in.

"Hide us, for pity's sake hide us. We are pursued! The King's army are shooting our men as if killing rebels is a sport."

"You will all come to the vicarage, I will hide you there. Quickly! Oh, I see you are wounded."

One of the men bleeding heavily from a wound in his side was close to collapse. Two strong women supported him as the vicar led the exhausted men to the safety of his home.

SOMERTON

WILLIAM, TOM AND Matt Turle were happy to be alive. The shocking scenes of the battle would live with them for ever. They had ridden to Somerton a town approximately 11 miles from Westonzoyland. The journey had taken less than two hours. William's cousin Hubert Kendale was the vicar of the Church of St. Michael and All Angels. Hubert was a widower. Elderly but still spry. His children had all left home and he was happy to accommodate William and the boys, playing his part in the struggle.

"I have business in Bridgwater with the vicar of St. Mary's. I will leave it until next week; by then there should be a clearer picture of how the King intends to handle the prisoners. I will also visit Sarah and the boys' mother to put their minds at rest regarding your safety. In the meantime, you and the boys must dress as monks. I will let it be known that you are here to assist me with a project dear to my heart. I want to help the poorer boys of Somerton to read. I have eight boys in my class, but I have not been able to find the time to copy out eight copies of the Lord's prayer and the lives of the saints."

"We would be pleased to assist. It will give us something to pass the time." William said. The boys nodded their agreement.

***

ONE-WEEK LATER William and the boys were engrossed in the tedious job of making copies of the lives of the saints when they heard the sound of a horse clip clopping up the path. They all jumped to their feet. William was first to the window and confirmed it was Hubert Kendale. Matt quickly filled Hubert's pewter tankard with ale and Tom opened the door to the yard. Hubert was understandably tired from the journey and, upon entering the house, flopped down in the nearest chair. He gratefully took the tankard from Matt and when he had quenched his thirst he tried to speak. Instead he started coughing.

"The dust, sorry, just give me a minute." Hubert took another draught of ale.

"That's better. The road between here and Bridgwater is in a sorry state. There are men hanging from trees. Done of course to discourage another rebellion but it is a terrible sight."

"Did you get a message to our mother?" Asked Matt and Tom in unison. "Did you see Sarah?" William spoke at the same time.

Hubert smiled. He understood their concern. "Yes, to all of you. They have been told you are all safe. I have told both ladies they must act as if they don't know where you are. It will be difficult for Sarah as she will have to keep the news from Paul and Harry. There is mischief afoot. Some old scores are being settled."

"What do you mean?" William was looking worried.

"A rebel by the name of Adam Condick made his way back to Bridgwater and was hiding in his house. Six months ago, there had been a dispute between him and his neighbour over a piece of land. The rumour about town is that the neighbour's wife noticed Adam's wife buying pipe tobacco. She told her husband who told the King's men. Whether it was the neighbour or not, the result is that Adam was captured and is now in prison."

"A sad story. Clive was so right when he told me to lie low."

"William, it would appear that you must stay here for a couple of months. The news is that an assize has been convened at Winchester. It is said that 4,000 rebels are to be brought to trial. The assize will move on to Taunton where Bridgwater men will be tried. It could be months before it will be safe for you and the boys to return home."

"How many months?"

"I can't say, it's bad out there. Judge Jeffreys, who has been appointed to preside over the prosecution of the rebels is an evil man. I heard a terrible story about some young girls in Taunton. They were convicted of treason. The poor young lasses didn't know they were committing a crime. All they did was to present a banner and bible to Monmouth when he arrived in Taunton. One of the girls, a child of eight received a brutal tirade from Judge Jeffreys, and he sentenced her to prison. The unfortunate girl was so terrified that she is said to have died of fear a few hours later."

"A girl of eight, sentenced to prison?" William, Tom and Matt were shocked. No one spoke for several minutes, unable to believe that such a terrible thing had happened.

"Appalling I know. I have had some time to get over my shock, but I still feel upset. There is more bad news. Sir Samuel Gilbert has been hospitalised in Bath. I don't know the details."

"Sir Samuel?" William was concerned. "You do not know why?"

"Bridgwater is in chaos. There are so many of the town's folk devastated by recent events. Normally I would have pressed for more information regarding Sir Samuel, but it wasn't appropriate. I'm so sorry my return has depressed you all. I must cheer you up. I do have an amusing story for you. Do you know of Jan Swayn?"

"Yes." William, Matt and Tom all answered together.

"Well then you know what a fine athlete he is. He was captured and one of his fellow prisoners told the King's men that Jan was the best hop skip and jumper in the whole of Somerset. The King's men, mellow with drink asked Jan to demonstrate his prowess."

"Don't tell me!" William was already laughing.

"Jan took a huge jump, then disappeared into the darkness. By the time his captors realised what had happened he was long gone".

BARHAM MANOR

"WHERE IS FATHER?" Harry was close to tears.

"My darling boy, we must be patient. Your father had an advantage over so many of the other brave men who fought for Monmouth. Your father is an experienced soldier.

"Mother!" Paul ran into the room. "The King has ordered that trials must start immediately. The talk is that the King is convinced he must act quickly to avoid another rebellion. I'm frightened mother. All my friends are frightened. Some have lost their fathers, brothers, cousins. Some have their fathers waiting for trial. And we don't know where our father is."

"We must put our trust in God. Until we are notified otherwise, we must believe that your father is safe." Sarah knelt and put her arms around Paul and held him tight. She longed to tell both her sons that their father was safe but knew it was too big a secret for little boys to keep. Harry joined in the cuddle and she stroked his soft hair. Sarah was fighting back tears; it was so difficult for women she thought. Men faced the bullets, but women and children suffered the agony of waiting.

***

THE ASSIZE STARTED at Winchester on 25 August and then moved to Taunton on 18 September.

Seven Hundred and fifty men who took part in the battle of Sedgemoor were sentenced for transportation. Three hundred and four were hanged. The bodies of the hanged were spread throughout the county. Fresh corpses blowing in the wind beside the now decaying bodies of those hung a couple of months earlier.

William, Matt and Tom eventually returned to Bridgwater. Mrs Turle's delight in seeing her sons again was matched by the joy felt by Sarah and her sons. After hugs and kisses for William from his family, Sarah told the boys to play outside.

"It's wonderful to have you back, safe and sound but I have some terrible news."

"There is a strange atmosphere in the house, what has happened?"

"Come, sit down." Sarah paused "It's Mabel, her Ben was hung from a tree in Westonzoyland.

"Oh God no! Not Ben. Poor Mabel. Where is she? I must go to her."

"William, my dear, Mabel is dead. She was so overtaken with grief that she drowned herself in the Parrett." There was silence, the grandfather clock in the corner ticked away the seconds before Sarah spoke. "It was too cruel. She had suffered so much. First the plague taking her husband and baby daughter, then Joe kicked to death by a horse. Poor Mabel, Ben was all she had left." Sarah was holding William's hand, tears running down her cheeks.

"She had us Sarah. She had so many friends. Why? We all loved her; we would have looked after her." William spoke, his voice shaky with emotion. "Mabel drowned herself. I can't believe it."

"Her grief was too strong. She had rallied before and got on with life, but she couldn't do it again. Ben's death was more than she could take. I paid Percival Hunt and his sons to go to Westonzoyland and cut Ben's body down. He was buried in St Mary's church yard."

"Mabel?"

"My dear William, you know where those who take their own life are buried."

"The indignity of it. Mabel would have known that she would have a shameful burial. It just doesn't make any sense to me." There was silence, both William and Sarah were deep in thought. The corpse of a person who committed suicide was considered unworthy of a proper Christian funeral. Mabel's naked body had been buried at night, placed face down in un-hallowed ground at the crossroads at the west side of town. The body buried facing north to south, the opposite of the Christian custom of west to east. Her body was staked to the ground, piercing her heart, this was to anchor her spirit to the grave. Then stones had been placed on top of her corpse.

After several minutes William spoke. "I can't bear to think of her lying there. She was a gentle, kind lady. For her to end up......"

"William, I'm so sorry. I dreaded having to tell you."

"I understand, you know how fond I was of Mabel. I desperately need to go the shipyard, but I will stay with you today. You have had a tough time, haven't you? Why are you looking at me like that?"

Sarah had tried so hard to persuade him to leave the fighting to younger men. He had disregarded her pleas. She knew from

Cousin Hubert that William and the Turtle boys had been well looked after by his housekeeper. She was tempted to make an unkind remark but couldn't. She had her husband back safe and well. She smiled at his worried expression.

"It has been horrible, William. Everyday there was another woman broken-hearted as the news filtered through of the fate of their loved one. Every day a new widow, or a mother who has lost a son." Sarah's eyes filled with tears. "I am so lucky. Having you back with us is a gift from God."

"Sarah, we are both lucky, I'm lucky to have such a beautiful, loyal woman as a wife." William took Sarah in his arms and kissed her, he held her close to him for several minutes, enjoying the floral scent of Carmelite water, Sarah's favourite fragrance.

"Don't ever leave me again, William, I have been so scared. Even though Hubert assured me that you were safe I still worried you might be betrayed."

"I promise my soldiering days are done. Poor Bridgwater, so much depressing news."

"There is some good news, did you know that Sir Samuel had been ill?"

"I heard that he had been hospitalised. Hubert told me, but he knew no details of the illness."

"He wasn't ill in the normal way, I heard it was a deep melancholy. He is back home. Oh Paul, what has happened?" Paul had run into the room, holding his head.

"Harry hit me with his bat." Sarah knelt down beside her son and inspected the damage. William left the room in search of Harry.

***

THE NEXT MORNING, William arose early. He was suddenly

reminded that Mabel was no longer part of his household. Agnes Warren, who had been Mabel's assistant hustled into the breakfast room with a plate of sausages and some newly baked bread. William smiled encouragingly at the young girl and thanked her. He was pleased to find the sausages cooked to his satisfaction and the bread well baked.

Before William left the house, he returned to the bedchamber to tell Sarah that he expected to be gone for most of the day. He felt uncomfortable about leaving her so soon after arriving back home, but he had been absent from his business for far too long.

William's horse was already standing waiting for him. His servants were pleased to have some stability back in their lives now that the master had returned. William patted the horse's head and received a satisfied neigh in return. Moonlight was also happy to have her master back. She started off at a slow canter, waiting for the instruction to move faster. Just as William was about to ask Moonlight to increase her speed, he was hailed by the vicar of St Mary's church, the Reverend Hugh Staunton.

"Welcome back William, it's wonderful to see you."

"Good morrow Hugh, I trust you are well."

Hugh bought his horse up by the side of Moonlight. "You ask me if I am well after all you have been through. Yes, I am well, but you and I need to get together. Much has happened since you have been in hiding."

"I am aware of that, but I must get to the shipyard, ride with me, we can talk on the way."

William urgently needed to spend time with Edward Palmer, his cousin, who managed William's shipping company. The Barham family had been shipping merchants in Bridgwater since 1458 when piracy had been a hazard. The exporting of broadcloth, which had been an important part of the economy of the town declined disastrously during the war with France.

Williams's ancestor had gambled that peace would once again lead to a demand for Bridgwater cloth. He had purchased a sound vessel at a knock-down price from a merchant who had turned his back on shipping. The gamble paid off. Peace did increase the demand for broadcloth from France, Spain and Ireland. Prudent accounting had kept the business solvent. It had survived the lean years in the early 16th century when Bridgwater had been in general decline. The Barham family, concerned that there could be another decline in the export business, had expanded into ship building.

***

"I HAVE HEARD that Edward has been working all hours to keep the business going." Hugh's horse had fallen into step with Moonlight.

"Yes, Sarah has told me, I'm lucky to have such a committed partner."

"It really is good to see you William, you have shamed me. If I had been a younger man…..".

"Sarah has nothing but praise for you, Hugh. You have been a pillar of strength to the community. We all served the cause in different ways."

"A lost cause. Monmouth beheaded, Somerset a county filled with sadness and despair. We know many will be transported."

"How long are their sentences?"

"Ten years."

"My God, what can we do for them?"

"Maybe money will talk. We need to arrange a meeting with men of means. You know of Sir Samuel's illness?"

"Sarah has told me. I was greatly distressed to hear of his bereavements."

"He appeared to be his old self when he came to church yesterday, though Dr Macey has told me in private that he is surprised that the physicians in Bath discharged him so soon. William, I do understand that you will have to spend today attending to your business, but the community has desperate needs as well."

"Just give me today. Tomorrow I will come to the vicarage and we will put our heads together."

"Thank you, between us we must find a way to help the town. I know you haven't had much time with your family but will nine o'clock be suitable for you? There is much to be discussed."

"Nine o'clock it will be." William turned Moonlight towards his shipyard, and Hugh continued towards the town.

***

WILLIAM ARRIVED AT the vicarage promptly at 9.00 the following morning. The two men were in deep discussion when the maid Angela interrupted their conversation.

"Please excuse the intrusion, Mr Manchip, the town clerk is in the hall, he says he urgently needs to speak to you."

"Bring him in Angela." A worried looking man entered the room.

"I'm sorry to burst in but it's the King!"

"What do you mean, it's the King?" It was Hugh who spoke. Both Hugh and William were standing, looking at the visitor with alarm.

"He's coming here. What will he do to us?"

"Calm down Manchip, when is he due to arrive?"

"On Friday. He is coming from Bristol. The information I have is that he will inspect the battle ground at Westonzoyland then continue his journey to Bridgwater. We will need to show our loyalty."

"I have no doubt that he will have been told that it is only months since we crowned Monmouth King of England. You did well to come to us. How many people know of the visit?"

"All the civic leaders. I came to you, vicar. I need your advice. Sir Samuel is the major landowner, respected in the county and known in London. He had no part in the rebellion. I.....we... the mayor and alderman were wondering if you think he is well enough for us to approach him. By rights he should be part of the welcoming committee."

"Without doubt, but I understand your concern, however the learned physicians in Bath have pronounced him fit and when I saw him yesterday he appeared to be in good spirits. I am needed at the church, but William can you go?"

"Manchip I will ride with you to approach Sir Samuel." All three men left the house. Hugh to walk to church and William and Manchip to collect their horses.

GILBERT MANOR

The door of the great house was opened by Percy, Sir Samuel's butler. Percy hadn't seen William since he had marched out of Bridgwater and was relieved to see him fit and well.

"Sir Samuel is in his study. This way, gentlemen please."

Sir Samuel had heard the arrival of visitors and opened his study door. He thought he had heard William's voice and was delighted when he saw that it was William.

"My dear chap, so wonderful to have you back. What terrible times we live in. Manchip, William, please be seated. Wine or whisky?" Both men chose whisky and Percy served them before leaving them to their business.

"Sir Samuel, we have been informed that the King will be visiting Bridgwater on Friday."

"This coming Friday? Are you sure?"

"Yes, obviously we are concerned."

Sir Samuel did indeed appear to be fully recovered. He paced the floor, invigorated by the prospect of being useful to his community again.

"I must greet him. I have been presented at court. He will have intelligence of those who were involved in the rebellion and he will know that I was not involved."

"Thank you Sir Samuel, that is what I hoped you would say." Manchip looked relieved.

"I will be delighted to support the mayor and the alderman. Manchip, I will ride into town with you. We must waste no time. We will call a meeting in the church. The town crier must be instructed to summon the people. They must be made aware that they have to accept James as our king. There can be no trouble."

"Sir Samuel, many folk do not believe Monmouth is dead. They still hope......"

"I will address the assembly. I will tell them that I have received a despatch from London stating that Monmouth was executed at the Tower of London on 15 July. A ghastly affair by all accounts. The executioner botched the job. There will be no more rebellion. The survival of the town depends on us all bending the knee to King James". Sir Samuel picked up a bell and rang it. His butler appeared at the door. "Percy, our horses. We must ride to town."

The meeting in the church was a difficult affair. Even though the highly respected Sir Samuel's plea for unity was accepted, many felt the need to voice their displeasure at having to pay homage to the man who had beheaded their hero. After the voices of discontent were silenced by Reverend Staunton, Sir Samuel rose to his feet. "There will be free beer and wine for everyone on the Cornhill if the visit passes smoothly."

***

THE TOWN WAS full, even though many assembled despised King James they understood the necessity of appearing to make him welcome. Sarah, wearing her best day dress, was seated with her sons beside her. Harry, being only seven years old, was excited by the occasion. His older brother Paul was worried. He had a much better understanding of the significance of the event and was aware of tension between his parents. He had heard them arguing the night before and knew that his mother was frightened. She was afraid that William's involvement with the rebellion might be known to the King.

Suddenly the sound of trumpets could be heard, then the sound of approaching horsemen. "The King! The King! God save the King!" The town's people were on their feet, loud in their welcome. Sarah grabbed William's hand. "It's Clive, William."

"So, I see." Captain Clive Pemberton-Harvey was leading the regiment of guards accompanying the King. He looked splendid; his athletic body perfect for showing off the ceremonial uniform.

The official welcome was short, the mayor had been informed that the King did not wish to linger long in Bridgwater. As the mayor was finalising the formalities, Sarah saw that Clive had left the platform and was making his way towards her and her husband. William stood, forced a bright smile on his face, and offered his hand to his brother-in-law.

"William, Sarah, it is delightful to see you both well. Paul, Harry, so grown up!" Clive smiled at his young nephews.

"Clive, it has been months since I've seen you. How long can you stay?" Sarah was pleased to see her brother-in-law.

"The King is anxious to depart. I have only a few minutes. Sarah, I need to have a few words in private with William."

"I understand. Please give my love to Lucinda."

Clive nodded. "My apologies Sarah for my hasty departure, you and the boys must come to Bristol soon. William, walk with me." The two men moved away from the crowd. "I see you kept your part of our bargain." Clive was smiling.

"Well, it was in my interest to avoid capture."

"I am happy to see you safe with your family, but I don't have to tell you how sickened I was to see you in the church, a prisoner, a traitor. A man commissioned to serve as an officer in the King's army."

"I served King Charles well. I was injured in his service." William notice the edgy look on Clive's face. There was the sound of trumpets.

"I have to go. The King is leaving. Take care of your family. Remember where your responsibilities lie. Also, remember I helped you and there will come a time when I will need you to return the favour."

BRISTOL – THE HOME OF CLIVE AND LUCINDA PEMBERTON-HARVEY

"SARAH, IT WASN'T just Bridgwater you know. We had men executed here. And then all those men being transported. Very dangerous really." Lucinda Pemberton-Harvey, Sarah's older sister was fanning herself. As pretty as her sister, she was showing signs of aging, fine wrinkles were forming around her eyes.

"How do you mean dangerous?" Sarah looked puzzled.

"Well smallpox. Filthy men, all imprisoned together. The population was put at risk bringing all those creatures here."

"Lucinda really. Have you no pity?"

"Traitors. They deserve their punishment. The King was quite correct in taking a hard line. He needed to ensure there would be no more rebellion."

"You forget that William rebelled."

"No, I don't! I was appalled, shocked, when Clive told me of William's captivity. Did not William have any thoughts for the family? Not just you and your boys but our parents, our children. Clive's family? Sir Maurice is a member of parliament. Clive himself? He would have been disgraced if his brother-in-law was hung as a traitor! William was selfish, childish and irresponsible."

Sarah opened her mouth, ready to defend her husband.

"Sarah don't say anything! I don't want us to fall out sister, but I demand that you do not try to defend William." There was silence. Sarah stood up and walked to the window.

"The gardens look splendid."

"We have had just the right amount of rain for the roses this year, last year the display was disappointing. I will ring for some tea. Where are the boys?"

"They are having the time of their lives with your new coachman. They are helping him groom the horses. Their faces when they first saw him! He was the first black person they had ever seen. He is extremely handsome." Sarah saw her sister smiling.

"It's quite the thing to have a handsome black coachman. All the families of quality have one. They go for a very good price."

Sarah frowned. "You make him sound like a possession, not a person."

"Well he is a possession. Oh, here is Mary with our tea." A beautiful young black woman entered the room. "Thank you, Mary, you may go. I will pour." The maid Mary retreated, and Lucinda moved to the table. She picked up an elegant silver teapot.

"I know tea is an extravagance, but I find it so refreshing. Clive told me that he saw Sir Samuel Gilbert when he accompanied the King to Bridgwater. I was pleased to know that he has recovered." Both sisters were upset and struggling to keep the conversation normal.

"His sons sent him to a hospital in Bath. He benefited from the rest and from the spring water."

"Clive said he looks well."

"Indeed, he does. He seems to have recovered from the melancholy he succumbed to when his wife died." There was silence, then Sarah spoke. "It was terrible, she insisted on seeing him while he was still hanging there."

"Why didn't someone cut him down?"

"It was chaos, Lucinda. Absolute chaos."

"She was such a charming woman always interested in other people. A great loss."

"She is greatly missed by the people of Bridgwater." Sarah's expression was sad. "Poor Sir Samuel, a son hanged, and then his wife dead by her own hand."

"I was told he found her."

"Yes. Poor man."

"Sarah, we both need another bowl of tea. We must talk of more pleasant matters. Then we will go and find Paul and Harry. I don't want my handsome coachman worn out by those little imps."

***

THE FOLLOWING MORNING Sarah rose early. She put her head around the door of the room where her sons were sleeping. They were both fast asleep. Sarah had noticed a change in Paul and Harry. They had become normal little boys again, away from the doom ridden atmosphere of Bridgwater.

Sarah moved quietly through the house, aware that servants were already up and working. She slipped out of the back door and walked round to the front of the house to admire the roses she had seen from the window. Dew was still clinging to the spectacular blooms. There were many different varieties and colours. The rose beds were the main feature in Lucinda's garden, but the events of the last months had led to the plants being neglected. Their gardener had not been seen since the day he marched out of town with Monmouth. Tobias was a thoughtful young man who took pride in the delightful gardens he created. The thought of him being dead, injured or transported bought tears to Sarah's eyes. She turned away from the roses and the memory they had inspired.

As Sarah walked towards the lake, she stopped, she could see the figure of Mary, the maid. She was running. Following her was a man. Sarah picked up her skirts and ran after them. They had both run into the vegetable garden behind the house. When Sarah arrived in the garden they were nowhere to be seen. Then she saw the garden hut. She heard a muffled scream, then a call.

"Help, help me!" Then a louder scream and a man's voice.

"No one will help you; you will do as I say."

Sarah pulled open the door and saw the man on top of Mary. "Get off her, now!" The man turned, horrified to see Sarah standing there. Mary rolled out from under him, and adjusted her skirts, her face wet with tears, her cheek red from a heavy slap. The man shuffled past Sarah and was gone.

"Mary you poor child." Sarah helped Mary to her feet.

"Thank you, Missus." Then she broke into uncontrollable sobbing. The attempted rape was just another indignity forced on her since her captivity three years earlier.

***

SARAH WAS STILL furious when she entered the breakfast room and found Lucinda waiting for her.

"Sarah, whatever has happened, you look distressed."

"I found a man attempting to rape Mary."

"What! Where..... who was the man? Is Mary alright? She is such a sweet girl. Where is she now?"

"Mary is in her room. I was walking in the garden when I saw her being chased. I followed and arrived just in time. I took it upon myself to allow her to go back to bed. She is badly shaken and has a cut to her face. The man must have been wearing a ring when he hit her."

"Sarah, describe the man."

"Mary told me his name – Andrew Broadbeare."

"Oh no not Broadbeare! This is terrible. I do not like him at all, but he was an army man, Clive's personal servant until he was injured. They are very close. Clive must not hear of this."

"Surely you are not going to protect an animal like that?"

"I have no choice. Sarah. I am horrified by what you have told me but sometimes it is better not to interfere. I don't think Clive would believe me if I told him. I will have to sell Mary. It is the only way."

"I don't understand why you just can't dismiss Broadbeare, Lucinda. Clive wouldn't condone his behaviour."

"I can't, Sarah. It's just not possible."

"Then I will buy Mary."

BARHAM MANOR

"YOU DID THE right thing. Poor child, how old do you think she is?" William had settled down for the evening, a glass of wine in his hand.

"Mary is 14. She has a workable knowledge of English. She was eleven when she was captured. Lucinda was sorry to lose her, but, as I explained, she felt she had no choice."

"Sarah, I am fond of your sister and I respect Clive as a fine army officer. But, as we both know, Clive's father is a slaver. Your brother-in-law's family's wealth is built on the backs of slaves. I am comforted by the knowledge that it will be Clive's older brother who will inherit the dreadful business."

"Lucinda told me Clive's father has purchased more land in Jamaica, and another consignment of slaves to work the land."

"We live in terrible times Sarah......" William hesitated. Sarah looked up from her embroidery. "What is it?"

"James Plomer. He was found dead. Drowned himself in the Parrett."

"Another suicide! James Plomer! I can't believe it. James would never commit suicide."

"He has been very down since Winifred died. But yes, I agree with you. He was devout; he would never bring the shame of a night funeral on his family."

"So, what are you saying?"

"It's not just me who's saying it. Hugh Staunton told me that James was one of the most devout of his congregation. Hugh was never convinced that Mabel would kill herself, and now James. I met up with Hugh and Sir Samuel and we are all of the opinion that someone is using the chaos of recent months to cover murders. Sir Samuel has spoken to the watchman and told him of our suspicions."

"Murders! So much death. I can't wait for this year to end." Then turning as the door opened, "Jessie, what is it?"

"Sir Samuel Gilbert, madam." The maid Jessie left the room and the rotund figure of Sir Samuel entered. He was flushed and agitated.

"Sarah, William, forgive this intrusion but I have information regarding those poor souls who are to be transported." Sir Samuel was waving a piece of paper.

"Please take a seat, a glass of wine?" Sir Samuel nodded, and William rose, filled a glass with what he knew was Sir Samuel's favourite wine and handed it to him. Sir Samuel took a few moments to savour the wine before opening the document.

"We don't have the names yet, but I have a contact in Weymouth, and he has given me the following information." Sir Samuel proceeded to read from the list.

"Ship Happy Return, let us hope for the men the name is a good omen. Destination Barbados 95 men."

Sarah gasped. "How awful."

"It gets much worse." Sir Samuel took another sip of wine, then continued.

"Ship Jamaica Merchant 162.

Ship Betty 80.

Ship John 98 men.

Ship Rebecca 14.

Ship Constant Richard destination Jamaica 90 men.

Ship Port Royal Merchant 120.

Ship Endeavour destination Leeward Islands 104 men.

My contact has told me that the King has already sold many of the prisoners. The queen was given 100, their value being £1,000. Those not already sold will be when they arrive at their destinations. The plantation owners will be delighted. There will be skilled tradesmen transported from Somerset to be their slaves."

"King James has a reputation for miserliness. He has saved on the cost of an execution. By a quick calculation of the numbers you read out, I estimate it's close to 800 men. Providing ropes, firewood, tar and salt for 800 executions for High Treason would amount to a pretty penny. Instead of spending money, King James is making money." William was indignant. He was suddenly aware of Sarah's distress.

"My dear, I will take Sir Samuel to my study, and leave you to your needlework. Sir Samuel, I will bring the bottle with us." The two men left the room. Sarah followed them, now disinterested in her embroidery and went to find Paul and Harry. They were playing soldiers.

WEYMOUTH APRIL 1686

"MY GRANDFATHER'S NAME was John." George Carrow was already feeling seasick and the ship John was still in port.

"They can't squeeze in anymore, can they? I'm beginning to think I would have preferred hanging. At least it would have been over quickly. The smell, George it's disgusting, and we haven't even started on the voyage." Thomas Dennis looked close to tears. "If only we had been further back, those at the end of the line managed to escape."

"We had bad luck; the soldier supervising us was a mean bastard. Thomas, that seaman, you know the one who gave us a drink of water, he told me that some men are so ill that there is no hope of them recovering. They are going to leave them behind to die."

"I'm not going to make it George. I have lost interest in living."

"Thomas, we are in this together. We joined up together and fought together and we will survive this if we stick together. I need you, Thomas, don't let me down."

It took eight weeks for the John to travel from Weymouth to Barbados. During the voyage many died. The conditions were appalling. The prisoners were crammed between decks, shackled to their bunks. They had little water, food, air or sanitation. Prisoners and even some of the crew succumbed to a fever that broke out. George and Thomas survived, both were young and strong. Their close friendship a factor in them supporting each other and overcoming the deprivations of the voyage.

BARBADOS JUNE 1686

"So, this is it. Barbados. Our prison for the next 10 years."

"Cheer up Thomas. We are still alive. We have our health."

"I don't know how you do it George. You always manage to see the bright side of any situation."

"I'm like my mother, a born optimist. Now my dad….." George pulled a face.

The agent for Sir Robert Eastmount had bought George and Thomas. They had little knowledge of the lives of wealthy men but a prisoner who knew of the family told them that their owner had been mayor of Bristol and was now a Member of Parliament. He had a house by the river in Bristol, which he kept solely for matters of business. For his family home he had recently purchased a large parcel of land in Stoke Bishop where he had built a splendid house. He relied heavily on his Barbadian plantation to support his extravagant lifestyle.

The agent, Mr Moggridge, was a miserable looking individual. He had a mean, thin mouth missing several teeth. He had come close to smiling when he completed the purchase of George and Thomas. The bidding for them had been brisk, both were carpenters, and there was a demand for skilled men. They were lucky, if it wasn't for their skill, they would have been put to work on the plantation, backbreaking toil under an unrelenting sun.

They were given the task of building extra huts for a new consignment of slaves Sir Robert had purchased. They were both used to finer work, both skilled in cabinet making but accepted their first task with resignation.

***

"WE ARE TREATED better than the black slaves. We are allowed to work without neck and leg shackles." George and Thomas were enjoying a rest in the shade. They watched the men and woman from Africa toiling under the unforgiving eyes of the overseers. Every now and then, to their horror, they saw the overseer raise his arm holding the evil looking whip. Punishment was not for wrongdoing. It was to just part of the process.

"Sometimes in life, Thomas, you just have to thank God for your good fortune."

"Good fortune! Captured, imprisoned, and sentenced to 10 years transportation, dumped on a smelly filthy ship with stinking bodies squashed up against you. Disgusting food when there was some. Only fresh air when someone died, and they needed to open the trap to move the body. Then being bought by a rich man. Bought! Belonging to a fat politician. You call that good fortune? I think the sun's already affecting you George."

"At least we know why we are here. Those poor beggars were just scooped up, taken away from their homes, their families. Just taken. Not able to say goodbye. Just taken to be someone's slave. Working to make money for someone they will never know."

"Moggridge is bearing down on us. I think we had better get back to work."

"Hold on there." Moggridge called them back. "Where are you going?"

"We need to construct a sledge to bring the wood up to the building site." George explained.

"No, you don't! The slaves can carry the wood."

"It won't take us long. The wood is heavy."

"Shut up! You won't waste time on building anything other than that which you have been instructed to build. Go straight to the building site." Moggridge had an ugly looking whip in his hand and looked prepared to use it. George and Thomas did as they were instructed by the angry overseer. They worked hard for five hours, heavy, difficult work, in the burning heat of the sun, not daring to take a break.

That night they both lay in their beds, listening to the sounds of their exhausted fellow prisoners. Some snoring, some moaning, some crying. They dreamt of Bridgwater, the river Parrett, the green fields, the sound and smell of rain. They imagined themselves sitting in their favourite public house, The Three Mariners, holding a tankard of ale in their hands, enjoying the conversation of friends.

BARHAM MANOR

"WE NOW HAVE names of some of the Bridgwater men who were transported. George Carrow, Thomas Dennis, William Drew, Henry Meyer, Robert Teape, William Tiverton, Joseph Vinicot, John Wall and George Mihill." Sir Samuel was waving a piece of paper, he looked tired.

"Have their families been told?" William asked

"Hugh Staunton has taken it upon himself to carry out that sad duty."

"What is the news?" Sarah had entered the room.

"We have the names of the Bridgwater men transported. At least we know now that the men are still alive." Sir Samuel passed the list of names to Sarah.

"Reverend Staunton is informing the families. I thought we might call on them tomorrow and see if there is any assistance we can offer. Sarah?"

"Oh, sorry William, yes. We must do as you say. I came in to talk to you both regarding St Matthew's Fair. My group of ladies has decided that it should be a grand occasion this year to cheer people. Your news has quite taken the wind out of my sails."

"St Matthews Fair! Yes, of course, last year passed without it. Mrs Barham, you and your ladies have the right idea. This latest news makes it even more important to have a happy occasion to look forward to."

***

St Matthews Fair had been held in Bridgwater for hundreds of years. It was the high spot of the social calendar for the district. It was the one time in the year that farm labourers had the opportunity to travel away from the farm. Affluent families would rent a house in the town for a week and socialise with other people of importance in the district.

The fair was the place where men and women would offer themselves for hire. They would carry the tools of their trade. Milkmaids would carry a milking stool, shepherds their crooks and stockmen their whips. A servant with no particular skills would carry a mop head.

For many people, attending St Matthews fair was the only time they left their villages. It was the only opportunity housewives had to stock up on items necessary to run their homes. For farmers it was the time to buy and sell livestock. The town of Bridgwater would be bursting at its seams with sheep, horses, ponies added to the hundred or more stalls selling rolls of cloth, boots, shoes, coats, hats, pots, pans and tools.

It was a time for the young women of the district to wear their best clothes, dress their hair in the prettiest styles and hope they would find a handsome young man to dance with.

***

THE CARRIAGE RIDE from Oxford had been tiring; it was good to stand up. Arthur Staunton picked up his holdall and thanked the driver. He waved to his fellow passengers; they were travelling on to Taunton. He had enjoyed their company. Their spirited conversation had made the uncomfortable 100-mile journey bearable.

Arthur stood for a moment in the centre of town, enjoying the hustle and bustle. The banging of carpenters building stands, the mooing of cattle, the bleating of sheep. He had loved St Matthew's Fair when he was a boy, and even now, at the age of 24 he found he was excited. It wasn't just the prospect of the fair that was exciting Arthur, he was longing to see Eliza again.

He felt in his pocket. The ring was safe. Arthur smiled to himself. He hoped that tomorrow Eliza would be wearing the ring.

"Arthur!" Hugh Staunton had arrived on horseback. He dismounted, tethered his horse and walked briskly towards his son. He flung his arms around him. "Good to have you back my boy, even if it is just a short stay. Your mother has cook making all your favourite dishes."

"Father, it's so good to see you. How is mother, her leg?"

"Much better. All is well at home." Your sisters have done an excellent job in looking after Arrow. They have been taking it in turns to exercise him. You will be pleased when you see what excellent condition he is in. Good journey?"

"As good as it can be. I had some pleasant companions, so the time passed quickly. I am sorry it is going to be such a short stay but my exams...."

"Quite understood, my boy. Let us get on our way." Reverend Staunton untethered his horse, and father and son pushed their way through the crowd and walked the short distance to the vicarage. Before they had chance to ring the bell the door was flung open. Two excited young women fought to be the first to hug their brother. The family dog Lucky, a mischievous black and white terrier, was jumping between the sisters trying to grab Arthur's attention. Arthur heard his mother's voice, and together with his sisters he walked through to the parlour where she was sitting with her leg elevated. Arthur went to her and bent down beside her chair and embraced her.

"Oh Arthur, it's so good to have you back. You have been sorely missed." Barbara Staunton was close to tears.

"You look well, mother. I have been worried."

"It's just a broken ankle, Arthur. My own fault, as you know. You do have a silly mother!"

"Yes, I do, trying to climb a tree, really!" Mother and son were both laughing.

"It was a good thing there were no men around when she fell. The vicar's wife with her skirts in disarray. It was fortunate that I was there to make her look respectable." Arthur's sister Jane was pretending to be annoyed.

"I'm never ever going to live it down. I know that. It's a lesson for me. A hard lesson, I am no longer the agile young woman I used to be."

"You must take better care of yourself mother. Father has told me that you were lucky, the fall could have been much more serious. Please excuse me mother, I need to tidy myself, the road was very dusty." Arthur left the room, returning a short while later. He had just settled himself into a comfortable chair when the door opened, and the maid entered.

"Tea! Thank you, Angela." She turned back to Arthur. "I thought your visit warranted the expense of tea."

"I am indeed honoured, Mother. And cake! I am famished. Sisters, some tea and cake please."

"Just who do you think you are?" Jane and Anne chorused

"It's wonderful to have the family back together, is it not, my dear?" Hugh Staunton was smiling at his wife.

The doorbell rang. The family heard Angela welcoming Eliza Macey. Arthur stood up, looking wary, aware that his sisters were giggling. He felt a tight constriction in his throat and pounding in his chest. The door opened, and Eliza entered. She looked uncomfortable; Hugh moved swiftly across the room.

"Welcome Eliza, welcome to our home. Please take a seat. You know my daughters, Jane and Anne, my wife Barbara."

"Indeed, thank you Reverend Staunton. Mrs Staunton, how is your ankle?"

"It is mending, thanks to your father's kind attention. Eliza, a bowl of tea? We have honey cake, almond cake and oat biscuits."

"Thank you, Mrs Staunton. Mother keeps tea for herself and

my father. I was allowed a bowl on my birthday." Eliza's lips formed an awkward smile. "Tea and a piece of honey cake, please." Eliza still hadn't looked at Arthur and Arthur still hadn't greeted Eliza. Jane and Anne exchanged amused glances.

"Arthur has just arrived from Oxford, haven't you brother?" Anne was enjoying her brother's discomfort. Arthur shot an annoyed look towards his sister. He tried to speak and failed. He was aware that everyone was looking at him. Lucky, sensing his master's distress jumped on Arthur's lap and started licking his face. The tension in the room was broken. Arthur laughed, "Get off me Lucky. Yes, I have just returned from Oxford. Eliza, how are you?"

"I am well, how long are you staying?"

"I have to return to the university on Wednesday. I have exams."

"Such a short visit. But you will be at the fair tomorrow?"

"Of course. I trust you will also be attending?"

"Most definitely." Jane and Anne exchanged glances, entertained by the formality of the conversation between their brother and Eliza. They knew that Arthur and Eliza were more than just acquaintances.

ST MATTHEWS FAIR

A choir of local children singing for pocket money greeted the crowds entering the fair.

"All you who roam, both young and old,
Come listen to my story bold.
For miles around, from far and near
They come to see the rigs of the fair.

Chorus!" The children yelled the word, encouraging the crowd to join in.

"Oh master John, do you beware,
And don´t you go kissing the girls at Bridgwater Fair.

The lads and lasses they come through
From Stowey, Stogursey and Cannington too;
That farmer from Fiddington, true as my life,
He´s come to the fair to look for a wife.

Chorus!

There´s Tom and Jack, they look so gay,
With Sal and Kit they haste away,
To shout and laugh and have a spree
And dance and sing right merrily.

Chorus!

There´s Carroty Kit, so jolly and fat
With her big flippety flopperty hat,

A hole in her stocking as big as a crown
And the hem of her skirt hanging down to the ground.

Chorus!

The jovial ploughboys all serene,
They dance the maidens on the green.
Says John to Mary, "Don't you know
We won't go home till morning, oh.

Chorus!

It´s up with the fiddle and off with the dance,
The lads and lassies gaily prance,
And when it´s time to go away,
They swear to meet again next day.

Chorus!"

Many of the people watching joined in with the chorus, the young starting a new tradition and the older people remembering their youth.

As the children picked up the coins thrown down for them, the crowd parted for Mrs. Joan Gamage. Her deportment was that of a proud expectant mother, her swollen belly preceding her.

Behind her, her husband was leading a goat cart carrying five happy children. Many of the visitors to the fair knew who Mrs. Joan Gamage was and she and her family were receiving smiles and nods of greeting as they proceeded towards the children's entertainment area.

Seven years earlier, Mrs. Joan Gamage had been Mrs. Joan Briddle. She had been married to her husband Emanuel Briddle for four years. During that time Joan had failed to produce a child. Wife auctions were a common occurrence at St Matthew's Fair, and Emanuel had offered Joan for sale. James Gamage, a widower, had offered £4.00 for her. It was the highest bid and the offer was accepted. Within a month of marriage Joan knew she was pregnant. The amusement in the local community was such that Emanuel left Bridgwater and moved to Cornwall.

As Eliza and Arthur strolled through the crowds at the fair, they were aware of the many admiring glances they were receiving. Arthur looked dashing. The cut of his new jacket emphasising his broad shoulders. Eliza, her fair hair covered by a modest cap, was wearing a dress of dark blue. Arthur turned to smile at her. "We need to lose them."

"Why don't you just give them some money? There are so many interesting items for girls to buy."

"Oh, I suppose you are right, but I always seem to be giving my sisters money."

"It will be worth it if we can have some privacy."

"I agree." Arthur turned and saw his sisters standing a few yards away giggling.

"All right you two, I give in. Here's twenty pennies." Arthur counted out the money and handed it to Jane. "Now go away."

"Twenty pennies each." Jane and Anne looked determined. Arthur looked defeated.

"Agreed. But you must promise to leave us alone."

"We promise." The girls took their money and skipped off towards a stall selling trinkets. Coming towards them was a party of boisterous seamen. The killings, execution, and transportation of Somerset men had left far more women of marriageable age than there were men for them to marry. St Matthew's Fair was a good opportunity for seaman from foreign ports to have female company. The seamen were welcome. They spent their money and they made good dancing partners. The watchman had been charged with the responsibility of keeping an eye on the sailors.

Arthur and Eliza had waited, concerned that Jane and Anne might have been jostled by the raucous seamen. Then Arthur heard someone call his name, it was Tom Turle. He saw him and his brother Matt walking towards him.

"Arthur, it's been nearly two years." The brothers held their hands out in greeting. "Eliza, how well you look."

"Thank you, Tom. I expect you two will be very popular this afternoon."

"You saw the seamen?"

"They won't cramp your style. Matt. You are both much better looking than any of them."

"Eliza, if you were not already spoken for, I swear I would be after your favours myself." Matt gave Eliza a cheeky smile.

"We are off, we might see you later?" Tom asked the question.

"Maybe, enjoy the dancing." Arthur took Eliza's hand. "Why are you frowning Eliza, it was a compliment."

"Arthur, let us get away from the crowds."

"Would you like to walk by the river, it would be much quieter there. The music is rather loud."

"Not really, Arthur. I am sorry, but my new shoes are pinching me. Can we sit a while?"

Arthur looked around, searching for a seat. He saw a bench under trees just a short distance away and steered Eliza towards it. Eliza took off her shoes and rubbed her feet.

"You have such pretty feet." Arthur took her hand, "Eliza, there is something I want to talk to you about." Eliza turned her head away from him. When she turned back to look at him, he saw there were tears in her eyes.

"My dear Arthur, you have been away for such a long time."

Arthur felt sick; he could sense that his beloved Eliza had something to tell him he did not want to hear.

"We have never had an agreement, have we? We have just drifted from being friends as children into a more adult relationship. Our parents sort of expected....."

"Eliza what is it you are trying to tell me?"

"I have formed a friendship with the Honourable Stephen Rodway."

"A friendship?"

"Arthur, my dear, it is more than a friendship. He has asked me to marry him."

"And you. What was your answer?"

"I told him I needed to speak to you first."

"What do you want me to say Eliza. Why did you come to my parent's house yesterday?"

"They asked me. They expected me to be there. To have not accepted the invitation would have seemed strange."

"Do you love him?"

"Yes, Arthur. I do."

William felt the ring box in his pocket. He felt ridiculous in his new jacket. What a fool he had been.

"Is he here?"

"Yes"

"Your feet aren't hurting are they? You just needed to talk me. Well Eliza put your shoes on and join your Stephen." Arthur's voice was cracking. He rose and stumbled off. Eliza sat for a while and then walked to the main gate where Stephen Rodway was waiting for her.

***

ARTHUR WANDERED AROUND in a daze. He was devastated by what Eliza had told him; he fingered the ring in his pocket. It was a warm autumn afternoon, and the fair had become even more crowded. All classes of folk were mixing together. The happy atmosphere after so much death and sadness led to well-to-do families socialising with the servants and farm labourers.

The sailors, full of joy at being on dry land were making the most of their time ashore. The vendors were shouting their wares. The auctioneers were trying to be heard above the noise of the crowd, the music, the vendors and the sounds of the livestock. It should be a great day to be alive, but Arthur was in despair. He stopped to buy a glass of ale, then another one, then a jug of ale. He didn't want to sit with the men who were drinking for enjoyment. He was drinking to forget.

Carrying his jug, he walked on to the river. He sat on the bank and watched the dark dismal water flowing past. Watching the water his sluggish brain noticed a tidal wave causing the water to rise. It was the bore; the water was travelling up steam at six miles an hour against the current. He stared at it for a few moments, he decided it was not as spectacular as the one he remembered seeing a few years earlier. He felt so tired. He finished the jug of ale and lay down to sleep.

***

"ARTHUR, ARTHUR, are you alright?" Arthur realised he had fallen asleep. He opened his eyes and saw the worried face of Molly Fisher looking down at him. Her green eyes complemented by the pretty scarf she was wearing showed concern. He sat up and looked around him.

"Molly, I am alright, I just fell asleep."

"Your sisters are looking for you. They are really worried."

"They are a pain; can't a chap wander off for a while?"

"They say you have been gone for hours." Arthur looked at the sky, he noticed the sun had moved much further to the west. "The afternoon is nearly past. I have slept for much longer than I thought. Molly, thank you for waking me. Um…" Arthur hesitated, he had a concerned expression.

"You know."

"Father told me. Molly I, I just don't know what to say." Molly laid a hand on Arthur's arm. "It's life Arthur, it is what happens. Your father has been a great source of comfort to me. He has shown me that my faith in the good Lord will give me the strength to survive. So many have lost husbands and children."

"Molly, I will pray for you. You of all people deserve to be happy."

"Arthur, Arthur!" familiar high-pitched voices caused Arthur to turn around.

"My sisters have found me. Will you walk with us?"

"No, I will sit a while. It was good to see you again. Jane, Anne as you can see I found your brother."

Molly sat and watched some children playing, then a man she knew came into view, Mollie waved to him and they had a short conversation. A courting couple passed her by, their arms entwined around each other. Then a young girl with a delightful puppy on a lead. Mollie didn't want to go home to her empty house, so she sat gazing at the muddy water flowing by. It had been a glorious September day, but as the afternoon was drawing to a close, she started to feel an autumnal chill in the air. She was suddenly aware that the children had gone, she was the only person sitting on the riverbank. Time to go home, she thought to herself. There was no one left to hear her scream.

Percy Collins, Sir Samuel Gilbert's butler stood on the opposite bank shocked by what he had seen. If he told anyone, they probably wouldn't believe him. He was not sure he believed it himself, besides Percy had his family to think about.

Percy wasn't the only witness. A slender young black woman stood shaking with fear. She didn't have the English words to tell anyone what she had witnessed.

***

ARTHUR HAD LINKED arms with his sisters and walked back to the fair. He was aware of their idle chatter but was deep in his own thoughts. He was surprised that his sisters were so caught up in the excitement of the day that they had failed to notice that Eliza was no longer with him.

At some stage he would have to tell his family that the expected engagement between him and Eliza would not now happen. He felt a lurch in his heart at the loss of his love; but talking to Molly whose husband Joseph had been executed for his part in the rebellion, had helped him. Molly had been stoically coping with the cruel death of her beloved Joe when tragedy struck again. She lost her twins to smallpox. If Molly could survive such misfortune, then he could be man enough to recover from his disappointment.

"We still have some money to spend. Arthur, please can you just sit there, I promise we won't be long." Jane looked beseechingly at her brother.

"I will sit and wait. Just don't forget we have to be back home for tea." Arthur watched as his sisters vanished into the crowd.

As he sat there, he saw a familiar figure, it was his godfather. Arthur stood, and raised his hand to attract his attention. He noticed his godfather was holding a brightly coloured piece of cloth to his cheek. It looked like a woman's scarf. Arthur was close enough to see blood on the cloth. He also noticed that the usually immaculately dressed gentleman was somewhat dishevelled. After a moment of hesitation, to Arthur's amazement, his godfather decided not to acknowledge him and disappeared into the crowd. The expression on his godfather's face was one of fear. Arthur started to follow him, perplexed by the old gentleman's behaviour, when he was suddenly knocked off his feet, he lost his balance, fell and hit his head against a tree stump.

A pickpocket who was being chased by an angry man had collided with Arthur who was now struggling to get to his feet. "Stop him!" was the cry from the man who was giving chase. Arthur tentatively touched the back of his head and looking at his hand, he saw the knock had drawn blood.

"Arthur your head is bleeding." His sisters had returned.

"It's nothing serious. Just a bang on the head. I will just sit here for a bit longer. I'm sure you will enjoy having some more time to look round." They both smiled brightly, leaving Arthur to touch his wounded head again. It had stopped bleeding, but Arthur had lied to his sisters, he was still seeing stars. He knew a knock on the head could be serious and felt worried. Concussion could cause loss of memory, and he had his exams to finish. Then he laughed to himself. Perhaps forgetting what happened today might be a good thing. It had not been the best of days for him.

BARHAM MANOR

THAT NIGHT MARY lay in bed unhappy for the first time since she had been bought by Mrs Barham. She loved living with the Barham family and the staff at Barham Manor had made her feel welcome. She had become used to the fact that her face was the only black face in Bridgwater. In Bristol there were many Africans.

Mr and Mrs Barham had made it clear that she was free and could leave them at any time. She would never leave them. They were paying her for her work and master Paul was helping her with learning English. Her tranquillity of mind had ended, she had witnessed a murder. She had recognised the murderer and she knew the man who had been standing watching. He had been kind to her when she had been sent on an errand. She had dropped the jar of honey she had been sent to buy. The man had purchased another jar out of his own pocket and sent her on her way with a friendly smile. She felt sure he would tell the watch-man what he had seen.

Mary shivered, she felt so alone. She wished she could talk to her father. The tears started to fall. Would she ever see her family again? What had happened to them? Were they still in Africa, or had they too been captured? She didn't know and had come to realise that it was unlikely that she would ever know. Mary cried for a short while, then she pulled herself together. She was aware she was lucky. Lying in her warm bed she re-membered the horror of the voyage from Africa. As she started to doze off, an English name floated into her head. Pacy? Perry? P it was a P, she just could not remember. If only her English was better, she could ask Mrs Barham, then she realised that in the morning everyone would be talking about the murder.

The clock in the hall rang just once, one o'clock in the morning. Mary was awake. The terrible incident she had witnessed was praying on her mind. Now she couldn't sleep. Her nightmare was returning. Mary remembered her home in the kingdom of Benin. Her name was Farai Ganazumba. The meaning of the name Farai was rejoice. Her mother had lost two babies before she was born, a strong healthy child.

Farai's family lived in the most remote and fertile district of Eboe. Her family's farm produced all kinds of vegetables, corn, cotton and tobacco. Farai remembered picking large juicy pineapples with her sisters. The whole family, mother, father, children and grandparents worked the farm together. Farfai could see them all, dressed in long pieces of muslin, wrapped loosely around their bodies. The muslin had been dyed a vibrant blue. The dye was extracted from berries. Farfai had not seen a shade so gloriously blue in England.

Farfai remembered sitting with the women of the family spinning and weaving. It had been a happy time. One of Farfai's brothers had taught her to play the drums and she had been looking forward to the next festival where she could accompany the dancing, singing and poetry.

Then word came that there was danger. People in a neighbouring community had been kidnapped. The farming had to continue. The babies would be carried on their mother's backs while they toiled in the fields. The children were all assembled together. Three young boys were ordered to climb trees and act as lookouts. Farfai was eleven, old enough to look after the younger children.

Several days passed, and there was relief as people began to believe the danger had passed. Farfai remembered the icy chill she felt when she heard the call, 'kidnappers!' The plan of having all the children together in a small compound whilst the adults were in the fields was disastrous. Before they knew it, the compound was under attack. Three armed men were rounding up the children. Farfai had tried to fight off the kidnappers, but she was too weak. She was overcome, her hands were tied, and she and her young charges were captured. The men carried the youngest children, and Farfai and three other girls were forced to walk away from their home, their families and life as they had known it.

They had marched for days, stopping only for food and water and to sleep at night. They took detours when lions, rhinos and cheetahs were spotted. Baboons ran along side, seeming to mock them and then retreating to the safety of the trees. There would be sudden downfalls of rain, the water falling on the dry soil. When the sun came out again a pleasant musty smell filled the air.

Farfai had never met people outside her own community. As they marched, they were joined by more captives. People who spoke different languages. Fortunately, the languages were similar to her own, and with patience Farfai was able to understand what the newcomers were saying.

As a group, they were traded several times. She remembered the humiliation, being prodded and poked, her mouth opened to inspect her teeth as if she was a horse. Money was little white shells, Farfai remembered that one time she was sold for one hundred and seventy-two shells. Eventually, after six or seven months of travel mostly on land but sometimes on water, they arrived at the coast. There was a new smell, the salty smell of the ocean, and the fishy smell of seaweed.

"Mary, Mary, get up lass, it's 6.00 o'clock. You're late!" Farai woke up, shocked. Cook was knocking on the door. She lay confused for several minutes, then remembered that she was Mary. Farai had died some time ago.

BARBADOS FEBRUARY 1687

ARTHUR WAS HAPPY to be on dry land, the voyage from Bridgwater had been tedious. He was still slightly mystified to find himself in Barbados, but his godfather had been adamant that it would be good for him. After disembarking, he saw the cargo being unloaded. Hundreds of bales of tobacco leaf were waiting to be taken aboard for the return journey. He noticed a miserable looking man wearing a large brimmed hat walking towards him. "Good morning, am I addressing Dr Staunton?" Arthur nodded, and held out his hand.

"Moggridge, I've been sent to meet you. I have bought a horse for you. Is that your only bag?"

"No, I have a trunk carrying my medical necessities. I am waiting for it to be unloaded."

"Wait here. I will arrange for it to be delivered to Eastmount House." Moggridge disappeared into the crowd of people either disembarking or waiting to embark on three ships that had arrived that morning. Arthur mopped his brow. The sun was burning the top of his head.

"All arranged. We need not push ourselves through the crowd, the horses are tethered over there." Moggridge walked off, Arthur picked up his bag and followed him. "Here Nobel, come on my boy, he's a bit on the spirited side but he will settle. You just have to let him know who the boss is."

"He's a beauty, he reminds me of my horse Arrow." Arthur mounted the horse, who whinnied and stamped the ground. "Can you pass me my bag? Wow, Nobel, calm down."

"You're doing just fine, he's always suspicious of a new rider." Moggridge mounted his horse and led the way, doffing his hat to a man who had just passed him.

They soon found themselves away from the commotion of the busy dock and settled at a steady canter along a dusty track. Arthur decided his first purchase in Barbados would have to be a wide brimmed hat. The sun was incredibly hot, and the bright light was making him feel dizzy. After ten minutes they approached an imposing ornate iron gate. A large black man opened it for him. Arthur noticed he had the initials RE burnt into his forehead, signifying that he belonged to Robert Eastmont.

He had a worrying moment when his horse Nobel became agitated by something. Arthur, tightening the grip on his bag, saw that a weasel-like animal had just crossed their path. Moggridge who was riding beside him saw what had happened.

"It's a mongoose. They are all over the island." He slowed his horse to walking pace and they made their way towards a magnificent house, painted white and green. Arthur was amazed to see a building of such quality. It was in the Dutch style so popular in England. It had a gable roof with finials, a wraparound veranda and many windows.

"Eastmount House, you dismount here, the boy will take your bag." Moggridge gestured to a skinny youth who took his bag. "Ah here comes Fitzpatrick."

"Welcome to Barbados! John Fitzpatrick." John held out his hand in greeting. Arthur struggled to keep a straight face. Smiling at him was a young black man; he was not as black as most of the slaves Arthur had passed during the short journey. John was tall and muscular, his eyes shining in amusement at the Englishman's astonished expression. John was black, but he spoke with an Irish accent. "Arthur Staunton, delighted to make your acquaintance John."

"John will be showing you around. I will take my leave. Good day to you doctor." Moggridge had turned his horse around.

"Come, I will get you settled, Phillip bring the bag." The skinny lad rushed forward at John's command. "This way, doctor. You will find yourself more comfortable out of the heat."

"You must tell me where I can buy a hat. I won't survive another day without one."

"I will have one brought to your room. Please follow me." Arthur was grateful to find that it was cool inside the house. He followed John down a long corridor to a pleasant room. "This is where you will sleep, the room next door will be your surgery. Do you want a tour of the house now, or would you like to rest?"

"A tour please. Then, would it be possible to have something to eat?"

"We will finish the tour in the kitchen, the cook is a good friend of mine, she will make something fresh for you. I will help you settle in today, but tomorrow I have to get back to work, I am a surveyor. I need to instruct two carpenters. Moggridge told me they are English rebels." John studied Arthur's face, trying to judge his reaction. Arthur stopped walking and turned to face John.

"John, I should tell you that I supported the rebellion. The town where my family live, Bridgwater in Somerset, lost many men to the rebellion. I feel guilty that I did not take part. My father insisted that my medical studies could not be disrupted. Can I ask you a personal question?"

"I suspect I know what it is." John was smiling

"I'm puzzled, you're Irish?"

"My father was, and I picked up the accent from him. There are many Irish on the island, and I speak to them daily, so I've kept the accent even though my father is no longer with us. He was shipped over in 1655 along with seven thousand Irish men and women by Oliver Cromwell. My father fought against Cromwell. He was classified as a rebel when he landed here, but he was also an educated man. He was useful to our present owner's father and had certain privileges. I'm the result of one of the privileges."

"So, you were born here. You are not African."

"Never set foot in the place. My mother used to tell me about it. Poor woman, she was only 31 when she died. She missed her mother; in fact, she missed her whole family. It's a cruel business, slavery."

THE NEXT DAY

"TOP OF THE MORNING to you." John greeted George and Thomas who had just been released from their hut. They had met weeks earlier.

"And the top of the morning to you, John." They replied.

"That misery Moggridge has instructed me to work with you. I have surveyed the site; we can start on the building today."

John, George and Thomas put in a good day's work. Moggridge dropped in only once to check on their progress then, satisfied with what he saw he left them to it. During a break, the three men fell into conversation. Thomas had mentioned that they came from Bridgwater, a small town in Somerset. John had said nothing. At the end of the working day, John, with a mischievous glint in his eyes, told them that he had a surprise for them.

"Come with me. I will introduce you to Dr Staunton. He has just arrived. I am sure he would be pleased to meet two English men."

"Where is Moggridge? He usually makes sure we are safely tucked up in our shed."

"He is over the other side of the island, you have a couple of hours of freedom, come, we shouldn't waste any time." John led them through the servant's entrance. It was the first time George and Thomas had been in the 'big house'.

They relished the relief from the burning heat they had endured throughout the day. They followed John down several corridors, then stopped outside a door. John knocked on the door and it was opened by a fair-haired young man. His face lit up when he saw John.

"Come in, oh, I see you have companions. Please...... I don't have enough seats for all of us. I don't suppose they expect me to have many visitors to my room. I will sit on the bed. Hold on, I can bring over the chair by the table". Arthur was animated, he was pleased to see the two English men. "John, you must make the introductions."

"Dr Staunton, I am happy to introduce you to George Carrow" George offered his hand to Arthur "and Thomas Dennis." Thomas crossed the room to shake Arthur's hand.

"The vicar at our church was the Reverend Staunton, I suppose you aren't related to him by any chance."

"What was the name of the church?"

"Church of St Mary."

"St Mary's in Bridgwater?" Arthur had an odd look on his face. He looked at John, who was struggling to keep a straight face.

"Yes, St Mary's Bridgwater – he's your father, isn't he? I recognise you now. My mother always helped your mother with the flowers. I sometimes came to help, and you were always in the way. They sent you away to school, didn't they?"

"Mrs Dennis? Yes, I remember her. My mother said she was much better at flower arranging than she was." There was a pause. Thomas looked sad, and all three men understood why. George decided to break the silence.

"Dr Staunton, what made you come here of your own free choice. Thomas and I didn't have any say in the matter."

Arthur smiled. "Please call me Arthur." Then he hesitated and looked embarrassed. "Well, I suppose the time has come when I can talk about it. It was a broken heart that brought me here."

"I didn't know doctors could mend hearts." It was George who made the remark. Thomas kicked him. "Idiot, you are pathetic George! Please carry on Arthur and excuse my stupid friend."

"Are you interested?"

"Yes, I know all about a broken heart. I got very drunk. Only thing to do." Thomas looked miserable. "You see, what had happened, I was working in Yeovil....."

"Thomas, let Arthur tell his story." John intervened.

"I asked my girlfriend Eliza to marry me. We had been courting for three years. I had a ring – a gold ring. I was a medical student, I had to save for a year to buy the ring." Arthur's voice had become emotional. George, Thomas and John were all looking sympathetic, guessing what had happened. "We went to the fair, St Matthews Fair. I was going to propose but before I could, Eliza stopped me. She had meet someone else."

"Same thing happened to me but how did a broken heart make you end up in Barbados?"

The Arthur continued. "You would know Sir Samuel Gilbert."

"Not know him, we didn't move in the same circles, but we did some work at his house." Thomas explained.

"Well, Sir Samuel is my godfather. He had helped to pay for my education. The week after Eliza broke my heart, I had to sit my final exams at Oxford. I passed. The original plan was for me to return to Bridgwater and assist Eliza's father who is a doctor, to learn more about being the communities' physician before he retired. I would then take over his practice. Obviously, that wasn't going to happen. Eliza was to marry Honourable Stephen Rodway. It would be a grand occasion and the Rodway family own a large estate in Cannington. Eliza would often be in town. I just wanted to get as far away as possibly from Bridgwater.

My father had told Sir Samuel of my situation. Sir Samuel was aware that Sir Robert Eastmount, the owner of the plantation had expressed a desire to have a physician on the plantation."

"To look after the slaves?"

"To look after him and his family when they visited and to look after people like you. Skilled men that they paid a tidy sum for.

So here I am."

"So, we should be grateful to Eliza?"

"Well, perhaps." Arthur looked uncomfortable. He decided to change the subject. "It is amazing that we all come from the same small town in Somerset."

"Arthur, I'm sorry to interrupt, but I think it would be wise if I walk Thomas and George back to their quarters. Even though Moggridge rode over to the other side of the island, he may well send his assistant to check that all prisoners are safely tucked up for the night."

"John's right, we must get back. Goodnight Doc......sorry Arthur. Its good to have another Bridgwater man here." They shook hands as they left.

ONE WEEK LATER

ARTHUR HAD ACCOMPANIED Moggridge who had asked him to check on the broken wrist of the harbour master. It was the first time Arthur had been to the docks since he had arrived. A ship carrying slaves was being unloaded. He knew that conditions on the slave ships were horrific, but he was shocked when he saw a group of men and women penned together in a yard. They were just skin and bones. They looked like walking skeletons covered with pieces of tanned leather.

"They won't bring much; it would cost too much to fatten them up for work." Moggridge was unmoved by the pitiful sight. They walked on to another yard where heathier looking African men were being washed, shaved and their bodies oiled to make them appear strong and vigorous. Arthur became aware of a group of women sobbing uncontrollably. Their children were being taken away from them.

Arthur said nothing to Moggridge but the next day he found John working on his own, drawing up plans for a new building.

"Arthur you are just in time to give me your opinion. What do you think?" John pointed to his drawing.

"It looks very professional, but I'm not qualified to pass comment. John....." Arthur hesitated; "I was at the docks yesterday with Moggridge. I saw the new arrivals. I was shocked."

"Sit down, Arthur. It's a depressing sight." John looked sympathetic.

"I'm ignorant of the process. How does the system work? Do you have time now?"

"Yes, I do have time." John sighed "It's a terrible business." He had a flask of water and he offer it to Arthur, who took it gratefully.

"The way it works is that the arrivals are sold and issued with a new name, a British name. They are then branded with the name of their owner. It is a fact that thousands of slaves have been branded with the initials DY on their foreheads. They were slaves purchased by King James when he was Duke of York.

"Thousands?"

"Many died and then they are replaced with more." John continued. "The separation of families and the stripping of their identity is a deliberate process, intended to make the Africans totally passive and subservient. It is a policy designed to break their will power. The enslaved Africans are then 'seasoned.' This expression means that for a period of two to three years they are trained to endure their work and conditions - obey or receive the lash. It is mental and physical torture. It is a life of endless labour. They work up to 18 hours a day, sometimes longer at busy periods such as harvest. There are no weekends or rest days. Arthur, life expectancy is short on many plantations, only seven to nine years." John paused.

"I came here for several reasons John. One of them was to understand just what happens to the slaves. People back home are ignorant of the true situation. Seven to nine years, slavery could be called a form of murder."

"You could say that Arthur. It's well organised. The hierarchy on plantations is set up with a white owner, a white manager, white overseers and bookkeepers. Then there are skilled black men, like me and carpenters/sugar boilers, coopers, potters, blacksmiths and distillers. In most cases these men would have learnt their skills in Africa before they were transported. Some would have been trained upon arrival. Then there are drivers; black men and women who supervise their fellow slaves.

Another category is household slaves; very often these will be of a lighter colour, the produce of relationships between the white owner and female slaves. Some slaves work in the town as boatmen or watchmen. Other jobs are on the farm; cattlemen and hog boys." John looked depressed. He had lived with the system all his life. He saw that Arthur was angry.

"The whole process is repugnant! The casual way in which slave owners just use men and women like an expendable commodity, to be replaced by another boatload of miserable humanity, is something I can't comprehend. The Africans I saw yesterday at the docks were being treated like animals not human beings with feelings, fears, hopes and dreams. I'm ashamed to be English, ashamed to be a white man."

"Then do something about it, Arthur." John looked sad.

"Who me? The son of a provincial vicar? You don't understand how British society works. It's the people with money, the aristocrats and the landowners who have the power to change things. They won't stop slavery because it's too profitable for them."

"I don't wish to be rude, but you have been educated to a high standard, doesn't that cost money?"

"I had a benefactor."

"Oh yes, I had forgotten, Sir...........?"

"Sir Samuel Gilbert. Now there is an English man who commands respect. He is looked up to by all who know him. He is a wealthy landowner, but he always has concern for the men and women he employs, and he supports the old and poor in our area of Somerset."

"A good Englishman?"

"Most definitely."

"Well Arthur, my Irish rebel father would not have believed such a person existed!"

BARHAM MANOR

"KING JAMES IS very unpopular. We are a Protestant country and the way he is favouring the Catholics can't be tolerated!" William put down his newssheet in disgust.

"Father, how is it that King James is Catholic?" Paul was now 12 and was showing interest in adult matters.

"A good question, my boy. King James was the second surviving son of King Charles I. When his father was beheaded by Oliver Cromwell, he escaped to France where he spent most of his early life. He became an officer in the French army. The many years he spent on the continent, where Catholicism is the main religion, influenced him and he converted to Catholicism."

"Is that why the Duke of Monmouth wanted to be king?"

"Partly, but you see Paul, I have explained to you before that Monmouth was the illegitimate son of King Charles II."

"Our teacher says that the Duke claimed that the King had married his mother."

"Paul, there are many people who believed that, I am one of them. Unfortunately, before he was executed, the Duke confessed that his parents had not been married."

"So, King James is the rightful king."

"So it seems, but many people are against him. I have heard talk that William of Orange, the husband of King James's daughter Mary and a good Protestant may be asked to come to England and claim the throne. Don't tell the boys at school Paul, it is just speculation at the moment and I'm not supposed to know of the plan."

"Father, the secret is safe with me." Paul was looking serious. "You will tell me if it does happen won't you father. I would like to be first with the news. It is usually Bartholomew Powell who knows what's going on before anyone else."

"Paul, I promise you will be the first person I tell. Now I think it is time for you to do your homework and then go to bed. Don't forget to brush your teeth."

"Father, did you know I'm the only boy in my class with a toothbrush?"

"That doesn't surprise me. They weren't invented when I was boy. Have you taken it to school to show the other boys?"

"Mother won't let me. Good night Father."

"Good night my boy."

As Paul left the room, Sarah entered.

"William, we need to talk about how Clive's brother Reginald's death is going to affect Lucinda and Clive." Sarah had started to train Mary to be her lady's maid, and her hairstyle lacked its usual elegance. William thought the less formal look suited Sarah.

"Quite right my dear, I have already decided we must travel to

Bristol. I am extremely concerned. We now have a brother-in-law who is involved in the detestable slave trade. I am worried that our family's good standing in Bridgwater will be affected by our relationship with slavers."

"When will you be free to leave?"

"I will discuss the matter with Edward tomorrow. He will be as concerned as I am."

"William, Harry is in his last term at petty school. Now is not the right time for him to miss classes."

"That's true." William looked thoughtful. "Mrs Turle loves looking after the boys. I will send a messenger tomorrow asking for her help. She will probably welcome a break. Tom and Matt are more than capable of running the farm."

"I will need to sort out my gowns. Bristol is always more fashionable than Bridgwater."

"My dear Sarah, I am not sure that is true."

"The circles my sister moves in are quite definitely more fashionable than our circle here."

"You could be right, but you don't need any new outfits, do you my dear."

Sarah crossed the room and planted a kiss on her husband's forehead.

"Maybe, maybe not." William sighed, and picked up his newssheet as Sarah left the room.

BRISTOL – THE HOME OF CLIVE AND LUCINDA PEMBERTON-HARVEY

"CLIVE, THIS IS the first opportunity we have had to spend time together since you rescued me from Westonzoyland Church." William was sitting with Clive in the games room; a family dog was licking William's boots. "Hey, come on boy, stop that. Clive don't you feed your animals?"

"Here, over here Samson." The dog obeyed his master. "It seems such a long time ago, so much has happened."

"You will miss Reginald."

"As children we were close, but we drifted apart when I disappointed him and father by not wanting to work within the family business, but you are right, I will miss him. Mother and father are distraught, and Reginald's wife is expecting another child.

"I did not know that. Poor woman."

"Yes, my disappointment at having to leave the army is lessened by the knowledge that my family need me here. Your move I think William." William and Clive were playing backgammon.

"If there is anything I can do to help?"

"Thank you for the offer, your glass is empty, more wine?"

"Thank you, but we will need another bottle."

"I hadn't noticed." Clive stood up and went to the wine rack. "Exciting news about William of Orange. Have you heard the latest?"

"I know only that he and his wife Mary may be asked to make a claim to the throne."

"I have heard that he is preparing to invade England."

"How good is your source of information?"

"This goes no further?"

"Clive, you have my word."

"Father was in the House last week. There is real excitement, many believe we will soon have a Protestant king."

"Let us drink to that, and to your new role as the head of the Pemberton-Harvey family business."

"William, thank you. It's good to have you and Sarah here."

Clive stood, contemplating the bottle in his hand. He looked uncomfortable.

"We have had our differences William, in the past you and I have not been friends, but the tragedy of my brother's untimely death has made me realise that family is important. My sisters, who I love dearly, do not understand my sadness at having to leave the army life behind. Their husbands are pleasant enough chaps but all three have what I would describe as soft professions, law, religion and accountancy. You William, had a career as an Army Officer, you understand."

"Clive, my dear fellow, it is a difficult time for you." William was surprised by Clive taking him in to his confidence. Clive opened the bottle and replenished their glasses.

"I do understand." William continued. "When I was injured and had to leave the army I was devastated. I too had to become involved in the family business although I had the advantage of having my cousin Edward at the helm."

"Father's distress at losing Reginald is bad enough but he is upset with me because years ago I insisted on joining the army. He now sees his business being run by a son who has no knowledge of merchant shipping. Mother sided with me, she said I should be allowed to follow in the footsteps of her own father and become a soldier, now she is suffering from father's simmering anger at a time when they should be grieving together for their son."

"Clive I sympathise, as I have already said please let me know if there is anything I can do to help." Clive realised that William had made a move while he was replenishing the wine. He was studying the board before he made his move.

"I have had a thought. You and Lucinda need cheering up. You must come to Bridgwater for November 5th celebrations. The town has the most enormous bonfire in Cornhill. People come from all around and there is a carnival atmosphere. Some folk dress up in the most outrageous costumes."

Clive took a moment to complete his move. He then turned towards William.

"That's an excellent idea. Thank you, I appreciate your thoughtfulness. Yes, it will do us good to get away from Bristol and my parents for a while." Clive picked up his glass of wine and swirled the red liquid around before he drank. "I've just remembered something I was going to tell you. Do you recall meeting the Hon. Peregrine Bertie at our wedding?"

"Was he the chap who was so gentlemanly when the serving girl spilt wine over him?"

"The very same."

"He was an MP?"

"Still is. He has been elevated to the position of Vice-Chamberlain of the Household."

"That sounds very grand."

"It is." Clive was smiling. "One of his duties is to be taken prisoner by the King on the day he opens Parliament, did you know that happened?"

"Oh yes," William laughed. "King Charles started the custom when he was restored to the throne. It was because the previous Vice-Chamberlain had played a part in the beheading of his father. Purely ceremonial, your friend will spend the day relaxing at the palace, but the King will have made his point."

At that moment, Sarah and Lucinda burst in through the door.

"Clive, Sarah has had a lovely idea, she said we need cheering up. She wants us to join them in Bridgwater for the November 5th celebrations. What do you think? We could do with some merriment."

"My dear, I think it's an excellent idea." Clive smiled conspiratorially at William.

"We will need to decide what to wear." Sarah nodded agreement to her sister and was amused by the expression on Williams's face.

"I will leave that up to you, Lucinda. Come ladies, take a seat, I will get two more glasses. You joined us at just the right time. William was beating me."

BRIDGWATER

"WE CELEBRATE THE discovery of the failure of the gunpowder plot in Bristol. King James 1st and his parliament decreed that the events of 5th November should be commemorated annually throughout the realm with the lighting of bonfires, but we don't do it in such style. I have to congratulate Bridgwater. It is indeed an exciting evening."

"There are two reasons for our enthusiasm Clive. We are good citizens and celebrate the failure of the plot every year. Bridgwater is strongly Protestant and the plotters were Catholic."

"And the second reason."

"We just like having a good time!" William grinned. "The town's people need an excuse to enjoy an evening of fun around a bonfire before the long, cold nights of winter really set in."

"What is making the fire burn so fiercely and why are you burning a boat?"

"Making a boat the basis of a bonfire is a good way of disposing of all the old boats we have clogging up the jetties. I am told up to one hundred tar barrels are loaded on board. Then any item that can be burned is thrown in. Last of all, they toss in an effigy of Guy Fawkes. That wind is a worry. I hope it doesn't get any stronger." William was frowning. His comment was heard by a man standing next to him who agreed with him.

"This is such good fun! I'm so glad we came." Lucinda was

hanging on to Clive's arm, her pretty face lit up in the light of the bonfire.

"Oh, hot potatoes. Who wants a hot potato?" A peddler was ringing his bell. He had roasted potatoes on a spade over the flames.

"Hot potatoes and a glass of ale, I think. Clive, perhaps you can help me?" The two men walked away. Suddenly there was a loud noise, then silence, then screams. Flames could be seen in the windows of a house close to Cornhill. A young woman ran from the house shouting. "My children, my husband, help, please, please...." She collapsed in a heap.

Clive and William were first on the scene and pulling their jackets over their heads, they boldly entered the house, but the heat was too intense, the smoke too thick. They could make no progress. They were joined by other men, carrying buckets of water they had drawn from the well, but the flames were engulfing the upstairs and refused to be tamed. The fire was growing fiercer each second and the ever-thickening smoke filled their nostrils. Sweat dripped from their foreheads and hot ashes singed their hair and stung their eyes. They had no choice other than to retreat from the violence of the flames. They found out later that they had failed to reach a man and two children who had been trapped in the inferno.

A team of town's folk had formed to carry buckets full of water from the well, and occasionally the flames would die down, only to be fanned alive again by the wind. "Get water from Durleigh Brook." was the call, as water from the well was running dry.

"Let me go, I want to die with them." Men were holding the young woman, physically stopping her from running in to the burning house. Tears were streaming down her face with the realisation that no one could survive in the furnace that only an hour ago had been her home.

A group of women had gathered around the distressed woman.

Children stood, some in tears as the merriment of the evening had changed to disaster.

"William, let me look at your hand. Oh William, we must get back to the house. You need to get this burn attended to. William?"

"I'm sorry Sarah, its Clive......" Clive had walked away, the thick smoke he had inhaled had made him feel sick. He needed privacy to vomit. Lucinda scurried after him, only to be waved away.

"The woman, where will she stay tonight?" William asked.

"In the vicarage. Barbara told me they would look after her. I will visit tomorrow to offer our assistance. Here are Clive and Lucinda. We must get home William, your hand."

"I hear you Sarah. What a tragedy. What a terrible end to a happy day. I have heard talk that a smut from the bonfire must have been lifted on the wind and had set fire to the thatch on the roof."

THE VICARAGE

"HOW IS MRS NORRIS this morning?"

"She is still sleeping. She cried so much last night that she must be exhausted."

"You will have to miss the service. She will be greatly distressed when she wakes up and remembers what has happened. She will need you Barbara."

Hugh and Barbara sat for several minutes in silence, then Hugh spoke.

"I can't believe those delightful Norris children are dead. I can still remember Jessie's christening. She just would not stop crying. Now she is gone. And to lose Nathaniel. The most able of blacksmiths. He will be greatly missed. How are our daughters? It was a shocking evening; I wish they hadn't witnessed the tragedy."

"They both cried themselves to sleep. So many children are going to be upset today. More misery for Bridgwater, just as people were beginning to recover from the catastrophe of the rebellion." Barbara dabbed her eyes with her handkerchief.

"Barbara, I will need to leave for church a little earlier today. I need to make adjustments to my sermon following last night's events. But I have been meaning to talk to you for some time about the girls. We must think seriously about their future. Jane is now 13, I married you when you were 14. I am concerned because so many young men died or have been transported after the rebellion. There are few eligible young men left in Somerset and a woman needs a man to support her."

"Hugh!" Barbara was annoyed. "Do we really need to talk about this now?"

"I have been dreading raising the issue with you, but last night's events have illustrated to me the need to make decisions for Jane's future, even if they are painful. Life can be so short; anything could happen to us. As parents we need to secure our daughters' future. We are not wealthy people, but if we get Jane settled then there will be enough money to support Anne should she fail to marry." Hugh hesitated before he continued.

"I think I should write to my cousin Jeremiah in Norfolk and arrange for Jane to spend some time with his family. There was no rebellion in Norfolk and Jane might find a husband there."

"But Hugh, Norfolk is so far away! I want my daughters close. I have already lost Arthur for I don't know how many years. You told me that the birth of a son to King James, threatening to create a Catholic dynasty has led to Mary and her husband being offered the throne. If that came to pass, then those transported will be pardoned, the young men will come back home."

"My dear, I told you there was a rumour, it's just a rumour. We must not be selfish. I would miss Jane, but it is her future we must think of. She will need a husband. Now my dear, I must prepare myself, I need a sermon that will ease the anguish of my parishioners on this unhappy day."

There was a voice behind them.

"The righteous cry out, and the Lord hears them; he delivers them from all their troubles. The Lord is close to the broken hearted and saves those who are crushed in spirit. The righteous person may have many troubles, but the Lord delivers him from them all; he protects all his bones, not one of them will be broken."

Hugh and Barbara had turned towards the door. Jenny Norris was standing there, holding an open bible. Her golden hair loose, her face pale and her cheeks wet with tears. Barbara crossed the room swiftly and led her to a chair. Hugh knelt beside Jenny. "Thank you, Mrs Norris, you have helped me with my sermon. Psalm 34 will give comfort to the congregation today."

BARHAM MANOR

"Hugh Staunton looked far from well. It was an excellent sermon, but I fear the strain of the tragedy has affected him badly."

"Sarah, I too noticed how pale he was. He was close to Nathaniel. He had conducted the children's bible class. Hugh told me that he and Barbara have told Jenny Norris that she can stay with them indefinitely, but he has written to Jenny's sister in Bath, they are close, so it is expected Jenny will make her home there. Poor Jenny, she has lost everything. Nathaniel, those beautiful children, her home – all her possessions. I must look through my wardrobe. We are about the same size. She will need dresses, underwear, a warm coat. I will go and see what I can find now. I can call in at the vicarage this afternoon. Lucinda, how is Clive?" Lucinda had just entered the room.

"He sends his apologies. He still has a severe headache from the smoke. He was sorry to miss church. I told him how moving the sermon was. It was brave of Mrs Norris to attend."

"She is a devout woman. She has many friends in the town, and she would know that it would comfort them if they all prayed together. Come in." The servant girl Mary entered the room.

"Excuse interruption sir, madam, message for you." Mary made a small curtsy, handed William the note and left.

"It is good to see Mary is so happy here Sarah. I do miss her. She is such a sweet young woman."

"We are pleased with her progress with English. She is intelligent and quick to learn."

"Good lord!" William had risen from his chair, visibly excited. "William of Orange landed at Brixham yesterday. We knew that there was a possibility that he would be invited to assume the English throne, but I had no idea that matters had progressed so fast."

"I must go and tell Clive. A Protestant king again!" Lucinda rushed out of the room.

"King James will fight, won't he William? More bloodshed." Sarah had a bleak expression.

"We live in precarious times, Sarah. God willing, matters will soon be resolved, and we can enjoy some years of peace."

THE EASTMOUNT ESTATE, BARBADOS

"AT LAST! I HAVE received a letter from my father. I so want to know how the family are, and what the news is from England." Arthur was excited.

"It's hardly news is it? It will be at the very least six weeks old."

"It's better than nothing. Just to see my father's handwriting comforts me." Arthur ripped open the letter and smiled as he started to read it. Then his smile changed to a deep frown.

"Father writes that Mollie Fisher is dead, he says she committed suicide. She drowned herself in the Parrett. I don't understand. I spoke to Molly at the fair. She was sad but positive. Her stoic attitude to her terrible losses made me feel foolish to be so upset about my broken engagement to Eliza. I just can't believe she killed herself. She suddenly disappeared just after the fair, but it was supposed that she had gone to stay with her sister. Then she was found caught up in some driftwood in the river. It seems that she had been dead for some considerable time."

"I remember Mollie, Thomas, do you remember her?"

"I certainly do. Arthur, when you say terrible losses, what do you mean?"

"Of course, you would have already been taken prisoner. Joseph was executed for his part in the rebellion."

"Joe Fisher – oh no! Why executed, why not transported like us?" George looked outraged.

"I don't know."

"Poor Mollie, poor Joe. He was a lovely bloke. Executed!"

Thomas walked away and kicked some stones. Then he turned back. "You said Molly had terrible losses, what else happened to her?"

"She lost her twins to smallpox." There was silence, broken by the sound of harsh orders being shouted at the slaves. "Molly would never commit suicide." It was George who spoke.

Arthur nodded. "I agree. There is something very sinister happening in Bridgwater. The Barham's cook Mabel Finnimore also drowned herself in the Parrett, then James Plomer."

"None of them would take their own lives. Our parents can't write so it is fortunate for us that you are here Arthur. Your father, the vicar, he must be concerned. Three of his parishioners committing suicide."

Arthur was scanning the letter. "Father writes he doesn't believe for one moment they have taken their own lives. Neither does Sir Samuel or the watchman. The problem is that with so many men either executed or transported, there aren't enough men to do the rounds of town and help the watchman.

There is other news, in June a son was born to King James. The threat of a Catholic dynasty has led to the King's daughter Mary and her husband William of Orange being offered the throne. If that came to pass, then those who were transported will be pardoned."

"Pardoned, we might soon be pardoned? A Protestant king! Then we will have fought for nothing. Just three years of a Catholic on the throne. I didn't fight for Monmouth the man, I fought for a Protestant king. We could be back home within the year. Just think of it, Thomas."

"It may not happen."

"It may have already, how will we know? When is the next ship due?"

"From England? Possibly in three weeks' time George. It may have some good news. I will make some enquiries tomorrow to find out when the next ship is expected, but now you must get back to work before Moggridge sees you chatting with me."

Arthur sat for a short while and read the rest of the letter. There was news of marriages, deaths and births. He was surprised to read that Percy Collins had left his position as butler to Sir Samuel. His father had written that Percy's daughter had a weak chest and Percy had decided to take up a position as butler in the Isles of Scilly, on an estate by the sea. Arthur folded up his letter and picked up his bag. He walked up hill towards Eastmount House. Thomas and George made their way down hill towards the new slave accommodation they were building.

That night in bed Arthur lay awake remembering the last conversation he had with Mollie Fisher. She had been sad but seemed positive about life; he could not believe that she had killed herself.

BARHAM MANOR

WILLIAM HAD JUST arrived back from the town. "Great news Sarah! The English army have changed sides and joined up with William of Orange's Dutch army. King James is left with no supporters. He has fled to France. What a wonderful Christmas present. Ah, I think I can hear Hugh's voice." There was a knock on the door and the vicar entered.

"You will have heard the wonderful news. King James has fled!" William had a broad smile on his face.

"I have indeed been informed of the King's departure; however, I am here on a grave matter. I have shocking news. Mrs Norris has been found drowned in the Parrett. Some people are saying it is another case of suicide."

"But you know that can't be!" Sarah had risen from her chair. "Jennie was to travel to Bath to be with her sister. It had all been arranged. Jennie was an extremely devout woman. She would never commit suicide." William was nodding agreement.

"That is what everyone I have spoken to believes. Barbara and our daughters are distraught. They were fond of Mrs Norris. There is concern in the town. It is the fourth drowning in the Parrett, all devout Christians. A meeting has been convened for tomorrow at 11.00. I presumed that you would wish to attend William."

"Yes, Hugh. I will be there."

***

THE MAYOR AND alderman, plus Dr Macey, William, Sir Samuel, and the watchman, Samuel Boyte were assembled in the meeting room in the Town Hall. The mood was sombre. The room was dismal at the best of times, the events of the past three years had delayed plans for redecoration. There was quiet muttering amongst the men. All were convinced that Bridgwater had a murderer in the town. The door opened and Hugh Staunton entered. He looked exhausted.

"Welcome Hugh, now we are all here we can officially start our discussions." The mayor addressed the meeting.

"Mr Mayor, before we start our deliberations, I have a statement to make." Hugh cleared his throat and coughed twice. "I have been at prayer since six o'clock. I have come to the conclusion, with the help of the Almighty that I cannot in all conscience bury Jenny Norris at night." There was a gasp from the assembly. "I have buried Mabel Finnimore, James Plomer and Mollie Fisher at night because of the disgrace of their presumed suicide. I am ashamed that I failed to follow my belief that they did not depart this life by their own hand. Jenny Norris had been living in my home for over a month, we talked about her belief every day. She did not take her own life. I will give her a decent Christian funeral, in the daytime." Hugh was defiant.

"Well said vicar. How many people in this room believe that Mrs Norris took her own life?" The mayor stretched his neck to enable him to count all the raised hands. There were none. "It will be noted that the meeting is unanimous, Mrs Norris was murdered by person or persons unknown. Vicar, I will make a copy of this minute. I suspect you will need it for the bishop."

"Thank you, Mr Mayor. I will write to the bishop telling him of my decision regarding the interment of Mrs Norris. I will also be asking for his guidance in regard to my other innocent parishioners humiliating night burials. If you excuse me, I will take my leave." The mayor nodded to Hugh and he left.

The watchman Samuel Boyte rose to his feet. "Gentlemen, this is indeed a melancholy moment. We have all agreed that there have been four murders committed in our town. I am without permanent support. My assistant was shipped off to Barbados. Tom and Matt Turle have organised a volunteer patrol made up of young farmers, but they all have their daily responsibilities and can only give a small amount of time. We do not have the manpower to patrol the riverbank day and night. Someone is taking cruel advantage of our weakened situation. We need to have assistance from the military."

"I will make an urgent request. Leave it to me gentlemen. We will have the culprit facing justice for the evil he has done." There was applause for Sir Samuel's statement, then there was excited chatter about the news that King James had fled to the safety of France.

Only four living people knew the name of the murderer. Two had been sent far away, one of them not remembering. One still lived in Bridgwater but could not speak English. The murderer was the fourth and he hated what he had done but believed his actions had been right. He had acted because he felt he had been called to do so. He hoped he would never have to kill again.

CHRISTMAS DAY, BARBADOS

"CHRISTMAS DAY IN hot sunshine. It seems all wrong." Arthur was mopping his brow. He was sitting by a long wooden table with George.

"Oh, for snow." said Thomas as he walked up with two slaves. "Can I introduce you to Bongani and Katlego." Arthur felt intimidated by the height of the two young men. Both smiled at him, their perfect white teeth contrasting with their smooth black faces. They were identical.

"You can call us Abraham and Matthew if it is easier. They are our slave names."

"Bongani and Katlego, have I pronounced them correctly?"

"Perfectly. Happy Christmas." Both young Africans shook hands with Arthur.

"Your English is very good."

"Thank you, we have been here since we were children, we were captured when we were ten. Master had us educated. We both work as bookkeepers."

"Arthur, they are far too modest. Bongani and Katlego run the finances of the plantation. Happy Christmas everyone." John had arrived.

"I was pleased but also surprised to find that the slaves are allowed to celebrate Christmas."

"Arthur, it is always a big celebration. The master is most generous. We also celebrate Easter." Arthur thought it was Bongani who spoke, but it could have been Katlego.

"The master is indeed generous, but my father always used

to say that celebrating Christmas and Easter gives the slave owners a convenient excuse to be lenient." John had adopted a serious expression. "He always felt that there was a darker side to the holidays. The slaves welcome the opportunity to be free to celebrate. For one day they can throw away the burden of their captivity. They can become human beings again. The slave owners know there is a constant threat of rebellion. The holidays serve as a safety valve. The knowledge that there will be a holiday to be enjoyed prevents insurrection among the slaves. My father believed that people like me, and you, Bongani and Katlego with our privileges are useful to the master. Slaves toiling in the fields see the benefits we enjoy and believe there may be a better future for them if they behave."

"That is an interesting analysis John, your father gave the slave owners no credit for their generosity. I have seen just how much food and drink has been prepared."

"Arthur, you forget my father was an Irish rebel. He had an extremely low opinion of the morals of English landowners."

"He is right about there being the constant threat of rebellion." Katlego spoke, then looked anxiously over his shoulder. John, who was sitting opposite, had mouthed something to him. Arthur also turned to see who was approaching.

"We need to change the subject. We are going to have to be on our best behaviour. Is it customary for the owners to be seen sitting with their slaves?" John nodded. "It seems that Lady Eastmount and her sister have decided to sit at our table." Arthur sprang to his feet. As the other men saw the two ladies walking in their direction, they also rose to their feet.

"Lady Eastmount, Miss Loveridge this is indeed an honour. May I introduce Mr John Fitzpatrick, Mr George Carrow, Mr Thomas Dennis, and........." Arthur hesitated. "Matthew and Abraham." All the men bowed to the women. There was an awkward silence.

"Gentlemen, please be seated. My sister and I wish you to have an enjoyable evening. Matthew, Abraham, how good to see you again. How you have grown! I remember so well the first time I saw you. I just had to buy you even though the price for you both kept climbing. It was so exciting!" Lady Eastmount was fluttering her fan. Matthew and Abraham smiled weakly, everyone else looked uncomfortable.

"Here comes the food, and rum for the men and wine for the ladies. Excellent, you may all start….. and I can hear music. How very pleasant." Turning to Arthur "Doctor I believe this is your first Christmas here."

"Yes, your ladyship." To the relief of the other men, Arthur took the burden of conversation with the two ladies leaving his companions free to enjoy the meal. All that was required of them was the occasional nod or verbal confirmation that what the ladies had said was indeed correct.

"I have received a letter from my father. He has informed me that there is a strong possibility that William of Orange may take the throne from King James." Arthur had been enjoying the rum and had inadvisably opened up a subject that should perhaps have been left alone.

"Indeed, we could soon have a Protestant king again." Lady Eastmount's tone should have warned Arthur.

"We were discussing the possibility that those transported as Monmouth's rebels would most likely be freed by William should he become king." Suddenly the others sitting at the table stopped their conversation. All eyes were on Lady Eastmount as she responded.

"There were contracts. Skilled men like Mr Carrow and Mr Dennis were bought for considerable sums of money. Sir Robert expected to have their services for 10 years. For them to be pardoned and returned to England before the contract expires would be unthinkable." No one spoke. They could all hear the merriment of the slaves as they danced joyously to the intoxicating rhythm of the drums. Slaves enjoying some hours of freedom, hosted by the grand Lady Eastmount.

"I want to dance." The Honourable Felicity Loveridge rose from her seat. Everyone looked surprised. The style of dancing was totally different from the gentile pirouetting customary in England. Arthur stood up, made her a mock bow, took her arm and led her to watch the dancers. The others sat, not knowing what to say to Lady Eastmount. Fortunately, they had only a couple of minutes of discomfort because a prosperous looking gentleman approached their table. He doffed his hat to Lady Eastmount, who looked relieved at the gentleman's arrival.

"Lord Plunkett-Browne, how wonderful."

"Lady Eastmount, I heard you were hosting a gathering for the slaves. I thought you might enjoy some more gentile company."

"Oh my, you are so right. Please...." Lady Eastmount rose from her seat and offered Lord Plunkett-Browne her arm. In a whisper, but loud enough to be heard she said, "I have done my duty."

"My sister's a cow." The Honourable Felicity Loverage's outburst shocked Arthur. She was standing looking at the dancers.

"She was certainly undiplomatic."

"Arthur, she wouldn't think it was necessary to be diplomatic. After all, she owns everyone sitting at that table."

"I am a little surprised that you found her comments disagreeable."

"I find Agatha disagreeable. I don't really know her that well. She is the oldest of the family and I am the youngest. There is twelve years between us. She married Sir Robert when I was just a toddler. She wanted a travelling companion and her children's education could not be disturbed. So, it was decided I should accompany her."

Bongani and Katlego asked to be excused and had joined the happy throng, twisting, turning and jumping. George looked at Thomas who shrugged his shoulders. "Might just as well, John how about you?"

"Come on, I'll show you how to do it." John led the way. Arthur and Felicity were still standing, watching. The slaves were looking at Felicity in her fine dress, smiling and gesturing to her to join them. To Arthur's amazement, Felicity danced into the crowd. There were shrieks of laughter as the young English woman lifted her skirts and swayed to the music.

The heat, the happy laughter coming from the exuberant throng, the thump, thump, thump of the drums and the effect of rum lifted the spirits of the men. For several hours they forgot the demeaning comments their owner had made. They forgot that they were just a number on a balance sheet, they, and the mass of people around them felt human again.

BARHAM MANOR

"SARAH, YOU ARE going to be so pleased." William was smiling.

"And what has caused that grin on your face husband?"

"Sir Samuel is once again indisposed."

"Not something you should be happy about surely?" Sarah was indignant.

"Not normally, of course, I wish Sir Samuel well, but he had been invited to represent Bridgwater at the coronation. It is important that Bridgwater is represented, after all, so many of our young men perished or have been transported."

"William, don't tease, what are you trying to say?"

"We are going to represent Bridgwater!" William grabbed Sarah and swung her off her feet. "We are going to the coronation!"

"Mother, father, what is happening?" William settled his wife on her feet and turned to see both his sons looking concerned.

"It's wonderful news, something for you to tell the boys at school about. Your mother and father will be representing Bridgwater at the coronation."

"Wow!" both boys were looking impressed. "That's just about the best, father, none of the other boys will beat that." Paul was looking at this father with admiration.

"Will you bring me back a toy?" Harry wasn't sure what a coronation was.

William knelt by his son, "We will bring back lots of toys, perhaps a toy crown."

"You know what my next question will be don't you William."

"I have anticipated it. I have ordered a copy of The Ladies Mercury. Apart from giving advice on the latest fashion, there are articles on delicate and curious questions concerning love, marriage and behaviour. I'm sure you will enjoy reading it. There will be advertisements for dressmakers. You can choose the one most to your liking. We will travel to London in good time for you to have an appropriate outfit made."

"William, I'm impressed." Sarah kissed her husband on his cheek. I must write to Lucinda. I suspect my dear sister will be a little jealous. Will we meet the King and Queen?"

"My dear Sarah, I can't promise you that we will, but I think it's a strong possibility."

"I must practice my curtseys. Oh, I'm so excited".

CORONATION OF WILLIAM III AND MARY II IN WESTMINSTER ABBEY

APRIL 1689.

There had never before been a double coronation in England. William and Mary had accepted the 'Declaration of Rights' which limited the power of the sovereign. They would also vow to maintain the Protestant religion. Roman Catholics were now excluded from the throne of England.

Mary was taking her father's throne. Just hours before the ceremony a letter arrived from King James warning her not to go through with the ceremony. He understood her obedience to her husband but wrote that if she was to accept the crown in her own right, while he and his new born son were alive, the curses of an angry father would fall upon her, as well as those of a God who commanded obedience to parents. Mary chose to ignore the letter.

The Archbishop of Canterbury, who would normally preside over the coronation, refused to do so because he continued to support James II. The Bishop of London stepped in and agreed to perform the coronation of the new king and queen.

Sarah and William had been pleased but surprised to find they had seats towards the front of the abbey. They had resigned themselves to being seated at the back. Sarah knew the time and money she had spent on selecting her outfit had paid off. Shopping in London had been a delight. She had been enchanted by the wide range of different fabrics displayed, linen and lace from Italy and the Low Countries, chintz and calicos from East India.

There had been accessories to select. Muffs that not only

kept hands warm but were useful for carrying handkerchiefs, money and perfume. She was amused to find that it had become fashionable to wear face masks, enabling ladies to move around the city without being recognised.

There were many different places where clothes could be purchased. Wealthy women shopped at the Royal Exchange and the New Exchange, but tailors, shoemakers, embroiders, glovemakers and milliners could be found throughout the City and in neighbouring Westminster.

Sarah knew that London women were thought to be more fashion-conscious than women from the provinces. Wearing appropriate clothes for such a grand occasion was very important. She was determined not to let William and Bridgwater down. Her final choice was a dress of fine linen in pale pink with a suitably modest neckline. It had puff sleeves with lace cuffs. She worn a neat lace bonnet, fur stole and carried a matching muff.

The ceremony was long, having two monarchs meant much repetition of vows. Sarah so admired the new queen. She stood and knelt then stood again as the ceremony demanded, at all times looking composed. Her husband, William of Orange on one occasion discreetly adjusted the heavy crown that had been placed on his wife's head.

After the ceremony there was a reception for the guests. The butlers from the grand houses had travelled with their masters and were a welcome addition to the staff working to ensure the large number of guests were being served with speed.

William was astonished when he saw a familiar figure walking towards him carrying a tray of drinks. "It's Percy, look Sarah, Percy Collins."

Percy's face broke into an enormous smile when he saw William and Sarah, he acknowledged them, pushed on through the crowd, delivered the drinks to the waiting guests, and then returned.

"We thought you were on the Isles of Scilly." William said

"My master, Lord Harcombe is representing the Isles of Scilly. It is a wonder to see you, Mr and Mrs Barham. How are your boys?"

"They are well, they are growing up fast. And your family Percy? We were told you moved because of your daughter's health."

"My daughter has benefited from the sea air. The boys are well, but my wife misses Bridgwater." Percy hesitated, he looked uncomfortable. "Mrs Barham, I hope you don't think me impolite, but there is a matter I need to discuss with Mr Barham."

Sarah and William exchanged surprised glances.

"It is a matter of some importance, and the coincidence of us meeting here has confirmed to me that I must speak."

William looked irritated. "Percy, this is a social occasion........" Sarah touched his hand, she whispered in her husband's ear.

"Percy looks distressed." She turned to address Percy. "I can see a withdrawing room over there. That would be a suitable place for you men to talk. William, I have just noticed Lady Bryon ...... ah, she has seen me and waved me over." With a smile Sarah had moved away and was lost in the crowd. William and Percy made their way to the empty room.

"God moves in mysterious ways." William looked alarmed at Percy's statement. He waited for Percy to continue.

"Mr Barham, my family worked for the Gilbert family for four generations." William nodded, he started to feel apprehensive.

"My daughter, as you know has always been a sickly child. Sir Samuel's suggestion that I should leave his service and join the household of Lord Harcombe was welcomed by my wife and by me. Our daughter's health is of the upmost importance to both of us." William nodded, and waited for Percy to continue. Percy was obviously having difficulty in coming to the crux of the matter. William could hear the noise of the party. He had left his drink on the table. He was starting to feel irritated again.

"Seeing you here, both of us in London, in the same place at the same time must have a meaning. It was destined that we should meet."

"Percy, I should return to the reception. Won't you be missed?"

"I saw something. I didn't tell anyone. I had my family to think of."

A few minutes later William left the withdrawing room in a daze. His drink was still on the table where he had left it. He picked up the glass and emptied it in one gulp. He coughed; he had drunk it too quickly. A passing waiter offered him another glass of wine, he accepted it gratefully. He needed to calm himself.

William saw Sarah, she was sitting with Lady Bryon and they were deep in conversation, both with their fans raised conspiratorially, obviously passing on items of gossip. Then he spotted Percy making his way through the crowd of guests. He envied him. Now Percy had a clear conscience, he had made his confession. It was up to William to decide what he should do with the information he had just received.

BRIDGWATER

"I TOLD YOU there would come a time when I needed a favour, William." Clive was standing, his posture that of the military man he had been.

William's head was thumping. He had failed to enjoy one peaceful night of sleep since receiving the confession from Percy. Now his brother-in-law was giving him a difficult decision to make.

"I will have to consult with Edward."

"I thought he managed the ship building business."

"He does, but we are joint partners in both businesses. If I am to lend you the Robert Blake it is not just my decision."

"Does Edward know just how much you are beholden to me?"

"Yes, and he is grateful to you. But I must speak to him first. It is a delicate matter. Clive, you will have to promise me that you will not be using the Robert Blake for anything to do with the slave trade."

"She will be sailing to Holland and Italy. Her cargo will be coal, lead, woollen cloth and animal hides. We must have her, William. We have to presume we have lost the Pride of Bristol. She was seen in distress off the Bay of Biscay and is two months overdue. We are still waiting for the insurance. Our other ships are fully engaged. We have a contract for the cargo, we must have the Robert Blake." Clive was pacing up and down. William who had also been standing, walked towards his brother-in-law. He put his hand on his shoulder.

"Clive, I can see you are distressed. I owe you my life. Of course, you will have the Robert Blake. Come with me now, let us go and talk to Edward."

THE EASTMOUNT ESTATE, BARBADOS

"ON 17TH FEBRUARY 1625 Captain John Powell arrived at what later became Jamestown aboard the Olive Blossom. Sir Robert always invites the other plantation owners to dinner on February 17th each year to celebrate the arrival of the Europeans, and

Agatha will be the hostess this year in her husband's absence."
The Honourable Felicity Loveridge was sitting in Arthur's surgery. "You are invited, I'm delighted to say."

"Did you ask your sister to invite me?"

"Maybe. Please come Arthur. I can't bear the thought of trying to smile through an evening with the totally dreadful Plunkett-Brownes, Bagwell-Giles family and Hammett-Lacey family. Agatha has told me that the dowager Lady Wrentmore will be a guest. She's a sweetie, but old school. You know what I mean."

"So, I have to be subjected to their snobbery as well?"

"Arthur, you are brilliant with snobs. When Sophie Bagwell-Giles hurt her wrist during her visit last week I had to push my handkerchief in my mouth to stop laughing."

"You are cruel, Felicity. The poor girl can't help the way she was brought up."

"Yes, she can. I had the same upbringing, and I'm not a snob…… I'm not am I? Please Arthur don't tease me. Say I'm not a snob."

"You are not a snob, just a bit posh. Now go away. I have work to do. Tell your sister I accept her kind invitation." Arthur picked up his medical bag.

"Where are you going?"

"The plantation manager's wife has broken her leg. I attended her yesterday, I am pretty sure it's a straightforward break, but I need to check to make sure she is resting."

"Can I come with you?" Felicity looked hopeful. Arthur hesitated for a moment.

"You're a sensible girl, yes, you can come. You could be useful. The Standerwicks have seven children under the age of 10. Yesterday they wouldn't leave the room whilst I was attending to their mother. They are loud and boisterous. You could distract them, perhaps take them for a walk. There is a nurse maid, but she is useless."

"Arthur, the children were probably upset. How did the mother break her leg?"

"She tripped over one of the children. Don't laugh, Felicity, don't laugh!"

As Arthur and Felicity walked down the driveway, they were amazed to see some strange animals carrying the hogsheads of beer and wine to the house. They were bigger than horses, with long legs, a big-lipped snout and a humped back. Arthur called out to the man leading the animals.

"I've never seen animals like this before, what are they called?"

"Camels, they have been imported from Africa." The man was pleasant; he seemed pleased at their interest in the strange animals. He stopped his camels and allowed Arthur and Felicity to take a closer look. They thanked him and he proceeded towards Eastmount House.

"I wish I was good at drawing; I would love to send a picture of a camel to my family."

"I'm a good artist Arthur even if I say so myself. I could make a sketch for you."

"Could you draw a turtle as well?"

"If you asked me nicely."

Arthur smiled. "Felicity, I would be extremely grateful if you could be so kind as to sketch both a camel and a turtle to enable me to send the pictures to my family in England. Is that nice enough for you?"

"Thank you, Arthur. Very nice."

"My next letter to England will have the sketches and the colourful bird feathers I have been collecting. My sisters will be delighted. Thank you. We are here."

Arthur and Felicity had arrived at the home of Mr and Mrs Samuel Standerwick. It was an imposing residence, a smaller version of Eastmount House. A harassed maid opened the door to them. Even in the hallway they could hear the high-pitched voices of the children. They were ushered into a bedroom where they found poor Mrs Standerwick in a highly distressed state. Felicity had to agree with Arthur's description of the children.

"Mrs Standerwick, how are you today?"

"Oh doctor, I'm so glad you're here."

"Why is your leg not elevated?" Arthur was dismayed.

"It was, but the children…."

"Where is your nurse maid?"

"Taken poorly." A large lady with pleasant rosy cheeked face appeared at the door. "Doctor, I was just coming to take the children out for a walk. Poor Masie the nursemaid is laid low."

"I'm Felicity, I will help you with the children."

"I'm the cook, Ada, ma'am." She popped a curtsy. "It would be good if you could help, they are a handful. Upset, you understand." Felicity nodded her understanding. "Come on children, Ada and I are going to take you for a walk. The doctor needs to talk to your mother." Felicity took charge and shooed the children out of the room.

***

"YOU DID WELL. Thank you for helping with the children." Felicity and Arthur were walking back to Eastmount House. Arthur suddenly laughed. "You have a butterfly on your head. It suits you." Felicity shook her head and the beautiful orange and brown butterfly flew away.

"I feel exhausted, no wonder the nursemaid has taken ill. I have told Ada I will go to the house again tomorrow to help. They are lovely children, just very energetic."

"It's good of you."

"It gets me away from my sister and her stuffy friends."

***

ARTHUR HAD NOT been into the Eastmount House dining room before. It was painted green and terracotta, and the centre piece was an imposing table of dark mahogany. Impressive portraits of Eastmount family members covered the walls.

The room was cool, two slaves holding large fans made from palm leaves were keeping the air circulating. The windows had thick heavy shutters and he had been told by Thomas that the walls were three feet thick. Both Thomas and George had been greatly impressed by the standard of building when they had been called in to make some minor repairs to some of the dining room chairs. The skills of the African slaves who had built the house were outstanding.

The conversation at dinner centred on the new king and queen. There was much speculation about how long the monarchy would last this time, there having been three kings in the last four years.

The food was excellent. The meal started with a small serving of flying fish, then mutton from the island's black belly sheep accompanied by sweet potatoes, breadfruits, yams and spinach. The dessert was a heavy pudding of fruit laced with rum. It was too rich for Arthur. Even though he had enjoyed the conversation during the meal with the slightly eccentric Lady Wrentmore he longed for the meal to end. He was just laughing at a rather amusing remark Lady Wrentmore had whispered to him about Sophie Bagwell-Giles when there was a sudden commotion at the door.

"Doctor, you are needed!" The butler had appeared at Arthur's shoulder. "Mr Moggridge has been injured. He has fallen from his horse. It's bad, that's what the messenger said. It's bad."

Arthur was immediately on his feet. He reached for a pitcher of water, filled his wine glass and downed the water quickly. He had been drinking wine all evening and needed to clear his head. "My bag, I must have my medical bag!"

Another figure appeared in the room, all conversation had stopped, even the most inebriated had turned their attention to the intruder.

"There is trouble. The slaves....... they have pulled Moggridge from his horse." Samuel Standerwick was red in the face, his clothing dishevelled.

Felicity turned to Mr Standerwick, "I will collect the doctor's medical bag. You and the doctor can then hasten straight to Mr Moggridge."

"Excellent idea." Arthur called back from the door; he had grabbed his clean napkin from the table. Mr Standerwick hurried after him. Suddenly Standerwick stopped. He turned and addressed the room. "My men have rounded up the trouble-makers here. Gentlemen, I advise you to return to your plantations before the trouble spreads." He then turned and followed Arthur.

Arthur ran after the man who had raised the alarm. Moggridge had obviously been making his way to Eastmount House as he had fallen close to the gates. He saw John and Bongani both lying injured. John called out that they were alright. "It's Moggridge who needs you."

One look told Arthur that Moggridge had a compound fracture of his arm, he had lost a great deal of blood and was unconscious. Arthur covered the protruding bone with the napkin and applied pressure with both hands to stop the bleeding. He waited, continuously turning his head towards the imposing gates of Eastmount House, straining his eyes in the semi darkness, desperate to see Felicity carrying his medical supplies. Then, to his relief, he saw her.

"At last! He's lost a lot of blood. Pass me bandages, quickly" Arthur's voice was authoritative and calm. He could see the look of horror on Felicity's face.

"Will he live?"

"By the grace of God, he will. Standerwick, we will need to carry him to my surgery."

"Of course, doctor, the butler and I will carry him. You go on ahead and make preparations."

"Felicity, are you up to assisting me with the surgery?" Felicity squared her shoulders. She was trying to look more confident than she felt. "Of course, I will help......Arthur!"

Arthur turned just in time to see a dark-skinned man, the knife in his hand raised ready for attack. He had a ferocious expression on his face. Fear paralysed Arthur. He just stood, ready to meet his fate. He heard a gunshot; he saw the man fall.

THE NEXT DAY – EARLY EVENING

"IT WAS THE AKWAMU. They arrived in the last shipment. The men who caused the trouble were nobles in their own country; wealthy merchants, powerful members of society desperate to escape slavery. They are educated men. The other slaves look up to them." Bongani had a deep cut in his hand. Arthur had strapped it up for him. "They were arrogant. They know nothing of how things are here. We all want to escape, but now they have spoilt it for everyone."

"Moggridge would be dead if John and Bongani hadn't fought off the men who pulled him from his horse." Katlego passed the bottle of rum to Thomas. It was now easy to tell the twins apart because Katlego was wearing a bandage over his left eye.

"I'm lucky to be alive. If it hadn't been for Standerwick's quick action....." Arthur shook his head, remembering.

"We have made enemies. All of us. We stopped them when they tried to set fire to the new building. The Akwamu now see us as on the side of their masters."

"I agree with Thomas. We helped Standerwick's men fight the blaze because the new building is now occupied by slaves, which the Akwamu didn't know when they set fire to it. We helped Moggridge because he is always fair."

"You surprise me." Said Arthur. "You always call him Misery Moggridge. Whenever I see him overseeing the slaves, he always has his whip raised."

"Yes, but he seldom uses it. He is always miserable because he hates his job. Any decent man would. What the Akwamu don't understand is that if we had allowed them to kill Moggridge the master would have made all the slaves suffer."

"We are Kwahus, there has been bad blood between the Akwamu and Kwahus. Katlego and I are not safe here. We must find a way to escape."

"John, have any slaves escaped from here?"

"Yes Thomas, there was a large breakout last year, but all the slaves were rounded up. The escaping slaves were punished, poor devils. It was a horrible time. The slaves were hunted down by dogs." John paused. "Six of them were burnt alive. Eleven were beheaded……." John stopped speaking as the door opened and a gust of wind blew out one of the candles.

"Moggridge is asking to see John and Bongani, he wants to thank them." Felicity had entered the room. "Arthur, what is it? You look as if you have seen a ghost."

"Quick Arthur, sit down." Thomas pulled up a chair. Everyone in the room was concerned. Arthur put his head in his hands. He was muttering to himself. "I'm a physician, I understand what has happened. Traumatic events, just like those I have experienced in the last few hours can trigger memories." Suddenly he turned to Felicity. "Felicity, where did you get that scarf?"

"I bought it from a travelling peddler at a fair in Bristol."

"A travelling peddler? Could he have visited Bridgwater?"

"Yes, there are many peddlers who move through the West Country, visiting all the fairs." Arthur stood up.

"You will have to excuse me. I need to walk. I need to think."

As Arthur walked down to the ocean, he was accompanied by the high-pitched chorus of whistling frogs. His mind was far away from the exotic sounds of Barbados. He was back in Bridgwater. He knew where he had seen a scarf, a woman's scarf like the one Felicity was wearing. It was as if a fog had been lifted from his mind. He now remembered the fleeting meeting of eyes with his godfather, who turned away from him as if he hadn't recognised him. He remembered that it was the day Eliza had rejected him, and his mind had been in torment. He remembered now that he had been puzzled by the pressure his godfather had put him under to accept the position in Barbados. It had suited him; he wanted to get as far away as possible from Eliza. He had taken a knock on the head, which had worried him, distracted him from the terrible truth of what he now remembered. It was the day Molly Fisher died. It was Molly's scarf his godfather had been holding.

BARHAM MANOR

"WHEN I WAS in Bristol I saw the most interesting advertisement in the local newssheet. It was promoting an antidote to the possible poisons the African slave women may use when they are cooking for their masters." William was sitting in the garden with Sarah watching Paul and Harry playing with their dog.

"Really? Poison, they actually try to poison their masters?"

"So it would seem, my dear."

Sarah sat in silence for a moment. "Barbara Staunton told me yesterday that she had received the most depressing letter from Arthur. He wrote of the terrible conditions the slaves live in. Did you know that many slave women terminate their pregnancy or even kill their new-born babies rather than bring a child into the world to be a slave? They do it to rebel against the slavery system and, of course, they are depriving their owners of another slave."

"Slavery is inhuman. I have never understood why Arthur took up the position."

"Barbara said Arthur wanted to see for himself just how bad conditions are for the slaves. It was all organised so quickly, wasn't it? Arthur passed his finals and then was whisked off to Barbados. It was his godfather who found the position for him."

"Yes, ...it was." William looked thoughtful. He stood up and walked back into the house. Sarah was surprised at his abrupt departure.

BARBADOS

GREEN MONKEYS; turtles, butterflies, doves, herons, hummingbirds, whistling frogs, and lizards. Blue sea reflecting the blue sky. Sunshine, yellow sandy beaches and palm trees. Wandering on the beach, Arthur thought that the island of Barbados would be a paradise if it wasn't for the human suffering it contained. Arthur was desperate to leave. He couldn't risk a letter. What he had to say was so serious it would have to be said in person.

He had described his predicament to Felicity. She had been puzzled when he told her that it was the sight of the scarf that had jogged his memory. He explained that he had been knocked over and hit his head and had been worried that the blow could have been serious. Felicity still looked sceptical, so he told her about Eliza. Her beautiful blue eyes had darkened with sympathy when he told her of Eliza's rejection of him. She understood that his mind had been in turmoil. She confided in him that she had suffered a similar disappointment. The mutual exchange of romantic disasters created a bond between them, but Arthur was so wrapped up in his own problems that he had failed to notice that his suggestion of returning to England had troubled Felicity. She was a young girl, a young girl who was brought up in privileged circumstances, used to having her own way. She hoped Arthur would change his mind and send a letter. In her girlish mind, being separated from Arthur for what he told her would be several months seemed like a lifetime.

The aftermath of the uprising had made the volatile co-existence between slave and overseers even more dangerous. The rebel Akwamu people had been punished. Forty lashes each. All the slaves had been forced to witness the punishment. The rebels were being kept alive. Their scarred backs a warning to others and a reminder to them to accept the rule of their masters. Another shipment had arrived, bringing more of the aristocratic Akwamu. Bongani and Katlego were more determined than ever to escape.

Lady Eastmount's prophecy that Lord Eastmount would fight to keep George and Thomas for the 10 years of the contract proved correct. John was a marked man. In saving Moggridge he had killed a prince, the heir apparent to the Akwamu throne. The Akwamu would never rest until they had avenged his death. George, Thomas and John were discussing their escape ideas with the twins every time they had the freedom to talk.

BRIDGWATER

AT THE SAME time as Arthur and his friends were longing to leave Barbados, an elderly man was deep in thought. He had never meant any of it to happen. He had been a good man, an honourable man. It was the battle of Sedgemoor that had changed him. He laughed, not from amusement but from the selfishness of that thought. Sedgemoor had changed the lives of so many.

As he walked through the ruins of the castle, he was remembering the time 43 years earlier when Bridgwater was the scene of a fierce battle. He had just turned 21 and was down from university. He was thinking back to the time when he was a soldier in Cromwell's army when he heard the sound of voices and he was jolted back to the present. A group of boys were kicking a ball around, he recognised two of them, Paul Barham and Ambrose Vinicot, the son of the Hon. Richard Vinicot, his neighbour. They stopped their game when they saw him.

"Don't stop for me, I was just taking a walk-through memory lane, I remember the storming of the castle."

"We are going to have a lesson about Cromwell tomorrow, Sir Samuel." It was Paul who spoke. "Would you have the time to tell us about the storming of the castle? It would be good fun if we could impress the teacher with our knowledge." There was noisy agreement from the other boys.

"Nothing would please me more. In fact, I am rather proud of my memory of the battle. I used to walk my children through here and test them on their knowledge. Come, let us sit down on this wall." He took a moment to scrutinise the ruin. "It's safe enough. Now give me a moment to collect my thoughts." He waited until all they boys were settled.

"I was just was down from Oxford. My father had met me with the news that he had heard that King Charles had instructed Prince Rupert to arrange a meeting of those loyal to the crown in the castle, which was in the hands of the Royalists. My father and other major landowners were on tenterhooks wondering when or if Cromwell would try to take control of the castle.

It was a few months later that the Parliamentarian forces camped at Westonzoyland. Cromwell and his general, Sir Thomas Fairfax, realising the strategic significance of Bridgwater castle set up a plan to capture it.

In the Bristol Channel Royalist ships were intercepted to stop supplies reaching the castle. When reconnaissance was carried out it was quickly realised that breaching the wide and deep moat would be a major difficulty. It was estimated that the castle was defended by 1,800 troops and 340 guns.

"Wow, it's difficult to imagine. 1,800 troops." Paul was wide eyes.

"340 guns! How exciting. I wish I had been there." Ambrose was envious.

"It was a dangerous time Ambrose. Exciting yes, but seeing men injured and dying is horrifying. Something you will never forget. Now where was I? You have confused me." Paul looked at the other boys and signalled that they should not interrupt again.

"Oh yes, I remember the first attempt to storm the castle took place at night. By then I had joined Cromwell's army." The boys all looked impressed. "We used a large quantity of wood faggots to attempt to fill part of the moat. The moat was too deep, and the plan was abandoned.

Several days later a second attempt was made. We used floating bridges to cross the ditch from the Castle Fields side of the castle. The attempt was successful, the drawbridge was lowered, and the East Gate of the castle was under Roundhead control.

The centre of town became a battleground. At Cornhill and around the church, the Royalists own guns, captured by the Roundheads, were being used against them. The Royalists retreated and found that one part of the castle had been captured. Many of the Royalist troops changed their allegiance and fought with the Roundheads.

The Roundhead general, Thomas Fairfax demanded the surrender of the castle. The wife of the governor, Lady Christabella Wyndham who had been wet nurse to the King's son, Prince Charles appeared on the castle wall clutching her bosom. She called out to Fairfax "Tell your master that the breast which gave suck to Prince Charles shall never be at their mercy. We will hold the town to the last!"

The boys who had been sitting in silence now all giggled. "Yes, boys I know it sounds funny, but I can assure you that it happened, I saw her.

The following day the Roundheads set out to complete the storming of the castle. They first offered safe passage to the women and children who were in the castle. Eight hundred accepted the offer, including Lady Christabella.

In the resulting battle, the cannon fire from both sides resulted in fires breaking out all over the town, fanned by high winds. Eventually, Colonel Wyndham realised that he was fighting a lost cause. By evening, the castle was Cromwell's. I am not sure of the exact numbers taken prisoner, your teacher will know, but if I say 1,500 soldiers, 120 officers, several priests and two bishops it will give you some idea."

"Thank you sir, we now have enough information to impress our teacher." All the boys mumbled their thanks.

"Thank you for your interest boys. It's a great shame that you didn't see the castle before it was destroyed, it was a spectacular building." The boys left him sitting on the wall lost in his own thoughts.

He sat for a long time, remembering how it had been 43 years earlier. The town had celebrated. A town damaged but full of hope for the future. It was then that he met her. The prettiest, sweetest woman in the world. His Henrietta. The woman who would be his wife.

He stood up and kicked a stone in anger as he remembered the worst day of his life. The day after the disastrous battle of Sedgemoor news came to him that his eldest son had been killed. He had been executed by the King's men. His body was hanging from a tree, just one of dozens of macabre symbols of Monmouth's calamitous defeat. Unbeknown to Samuel, his wife Henrietta, alerted by the arrival of a horseman, was outside his study when he was given the news. She immediately grabbed a cloak from the hall stand, stopped to pull on her riding boots and headed for the stables.

After the messenger left, Sir Samuel poured himself a large glass of wine. He needed courage to tell his wife the terrible news. He would send servants to cut down the body and bring it back for burial. He finished his wine; and went in search of Henrietta. She was nowhere to be found. A terrible thought had occurred to him. He hurried to the stables where he found a stable boy busy grooming a horse. He alarmed the boy with his haggard appearance. "Have you seen Lady Henrietta?" The boy replied that Lady Henrietta had taken her favourite mare some twenty minutes earlier. She hadn't spoken to him, which was most unusual as she was normally friendly to all the staff. The boy said she looked upset.

With great haste Sir Samuel mounted his horse. His heart was bounding as he galloped towards the battlefield. He must stop her. She mustn't see her son. It was a sight that no mother should see. Rain had started to fall, all along the track bodies of once brave young men were hanging from trees, blowing in the light wind. Some already attracting the attention of crows.

He was too late. Henrietta had found their boy. She had cut him down, and with the same knife, she had ended her own life, and destroyed him. His grief at the loss of the sweetest, kindest, most beautiful of woman had left him in despair. He understood her anguish at seeing her son hanging at the end of a rope. Yes, he did understand, but it was grief they should have shared together. She had left him alone to grieve for his wife and his son.

He heard the church bell, he checked his pocket watch, dusted down his clothing and headed for the church.

***

TEMPERANCE LUKINS was desperate. Widowed by the Battle of Sedgemoor she had managed to keep her four children fit and well by working all the hours God gave on her small farm. She prayed for the day when her children would be old enough to give her a helping hand. Now the youngest Beckie was sick and she needed medicine. Her crops weren't ready for market. She was sitting by the side of the road, sobbing quietly. She had found a spot where she believed that no one would see her. She was a proud woman. She kept her troubles to herself.

Temperance was suddenly aware that someone was approaching. It was that sweet Mary, the pretty dark-skinned servant of the Barham family. They sang together in the church choir. Temperance quickly tried to dry her eyes, but Mary had already seen her.

"Mrs Lukins, you right?"

"It's Beckie, Mary she is sick. I'm worried to death……. I have no money for the medicine she needs." Temperance was dismayed by her frankness. Mary took a few moments, trying to understand what Temperance had told her.

"Beckie sick and you need money."

"Yes, that's right but I'm so sorry I should have kept my problems to myself."

"I have wages, Mrs Lukins, how much you need?"

"I can't take money from you Mary. I'm ashamed that I told you my problem."

"I have the money. It will be a..... what do you say..... I give you; you give back?"

"That's a loan Mary."

"Then, loan. Please take loan for Beckie." Temperance dabbed her eyes again. She then threw her arms around the slender body of Mary and hugged her tight.

"You are an angel, Mary. I will pay you back, but it will be in a couple of weeks. Do you understand?"

"A couple?"

"Sorry Mary, two weeks." Temperance hesitated. It could be three."

"It will be good." Mary smiled and nodded.

***

"THAT YOUNG MARY is an angel." It was a few weeks later and Temperance Lukins was sitting knitting in her garden, accompanied by her neighbour Mrs Turle.

"If it hadn't been for Mary's kindness, my Beckie could have died."

"Have you been able to pay her back yet?"

"No, it will be another couple of weeks."

"You should have asked me Temperance; I would have helped."

"That's kind of you, Nancy but I was too ashamed. I nearly let pride come before my daughter's wellbeing."

"When pride comes, then comes disgrace, but with humility comes wisdom."

"Proverbs"

"Yes, Temperance. You need to remember what the Bible tells us the next time you need help from a friend. Now my dear, I will be taking some sewing I have been doing for Mrs Barham over to Barham Manor tomorrow. I will pay young Mary. You can pay me when you are able."

"Oh Nancy, I would be so grateful. I feel bad about the delay in paying back the money to Mary."

"You don't have to worry about me. I have my boys to help me. You have had a hard time of it. We will say no more."

BARHAM MANOR

"THANK YOU FOR THIS. The needle work is exquisite. It's a present for my sister." Sarah was admiring Nancy Turle's embroidery.

"I need to see young Mary. She has done a great kindness to Temperance Lukins."

"Mary has? What has she done?"

"The youngest of the Lukins children was sick, real poorly. She urgently needed medicine. Temperance is too proud; she wouldn't ask for help. Young Mary came across her crying and Temperance blurted out her problem. Mary lent her the money."

"She's an angel that girl. She's always so kind. I will ring for her." A few moments later Mary entered the room.

"Mary, you did a very good thing. You lent money to Mrs Lukins." Mary nodded.

"I have the money to repay you." Nancy handed over some coins to Mary.

"Mary, thank you. You should be proud of yourself. I am proud of you. It was a good Christian act. Do you understand?" Mary, her cheeks flushed at the praise from her mistress, bobbed a curtsy and left.

"Well, I must get back home. I have two hungry lads to feed.

Please give my regards to Mr Barham." Nancy gathered up her cloak and basket and left.

***

"She did what?" William lowered his newspaper; he had been only half listening to his wife's chatter but now she had his full attention.

"She lent money to Temperance Lukins. One of the children was sick and she needed medicine." William rang the bell. A few moments later, Mary entered the room.

"Mary, Mrs Barham has just informed me of your kind act. I am delighted to know that you were able to help Mrs Lukins. She is a proud woman who has endured much since her husband was killed." Sarah and William were surprised by Mary's reaction to the praise. She looked as if she was about to cry. William had spoken slowly, to enable Mary to understand, but he was worried that she hadn't.

"Mr and Mrs Barham, you have been very kind to me. My English is better now." Mary stopped; she was wringing her hands in a most agitated manner.

"I saw something. I couldn't tell you. My English......."

William had an awful sense of foreboding. "What was it you saw Mary?"

"It was a man. He threw woman in river." Sarah gasped, she put her hand to her mouth, her eyes wide with horror.

"What! When did this happen?" There was a pause. "Do you understand Mary?" Mary nodded.

"The fair."

"Oh my God!" Both women looked at William in amazement. His face was ashen. The grandfather clock in the corner of the room rang six times before William spoke.

"Mary thank you for telling me. You know what you have said

is important. I have to ask you not tell anyone. Mary do you understand?" Mary nodded. Sarah crossed the room to her servant.

"Come, Mary, we will go and find cook. She made a cake yesterday. It was meant for the boys, but you shall have some."

When the women had left the room, William poured himself a large class of wine. He walked over to a portrait of his father and spoke to the familiar face looking down on him. "Now there are two witnesses. I must ride to town to talk to Hugh Stanton and see if there is anything that can be done."

There was a rustle of skirts behind him. Sarah was back. "William, what is going on?"

"My darling Sarah, I can't tell you. There is danger for Mary. We must keep her close to the house until the matter is resolved."

"She saw a murder. You know who it is don't you? There have been other unsolved murders, is it the same man?"

"I suspect it is."

"Tell me William!" Sarah was angry.

"I can't. I cannot tell you because there is no proof. A man's reputation is at stake. I must ride to the town and consult with Hugh."

"And if Hugh tells Barbara then she will know more than I do."

"Sarah! For God's sake this isn't a petty gossip competition! It's a matter of life and death." William pushed past Sarah, ignoring the hurt expression on her face.

***

AT LAST MARY felt free. For so many months she had fretted. She had been puzzled because she had never seen the man Percy again. She knew he had seen the woman pushed into the river.

She had expected the man she saw attack the woman to be

arrested, but he was free, still powerful, still respected. She worked hard at her English lessons. Young master Paul was patient with her, but his exams had meant that for several weeks he had been too busy with his own studies.

Mary had known that if only she could get to Bristol there would be Africans who had good English who could translate for her. She had hoped Mrs Barham would one day announce that she was visiting her sister and needed Mary to accompany her, but it hadn't happened. Now she had found the words. Now something would happen.

BRIDGWATER JUNE 1689

THE SERVICE HAD been moving. Reverence Hugh Staunton had been given permission by the bishop to commemorate the passing of Mabel Finnimore, Molly Fisher, James Plomer and Jenny Norris. Hugh had been able to convince the bishop that the deaths were suspicious. All four of the deceased had been devout Christians, regular and useful members of the congregation at St Mary's Church. A letter from Sir Samuel Gilbert had added authority to the request for a memorial service. The indignity of a crossroads funeral and all the unpleasantness accompanying it could now be erased. Re-internment into the churchyard at St Mary's would follow. The respect and affection for the deceased shown by the worshipers that afternoon had been a comfort to all who attended.

Sir Samuel knew what he had to do. It had all been a terrible mistake. He was ill. He knew that now. Deep melancholy had affected his brain. He knew God would understand that his victims had not taken their own lives. He had lived with the knowledge that his beloved Henrietta had been guilty of that sin. He understood all too well what it was to know that his wife had been denied a Christian burial. Until today, he had refused to acknowledge his guilt regarding the shame his actions had bought to the families of his victims, he could do it no longer. His befuddled mind had cleared.

It was the woman in the hospital who had started the horror. She had begged him to help her end her life. "The pain is too bad!" She would sob. "I want to die. It would be kind to let me die." The pleading didn't stop. The nurses and doctors were kind, but they could do nothing to help her. So, he did. It was an act of mercy. He just wished someone would do the same for him. Without his Henrietta his life was worthless. He had sons and a daughter, but they had their own lives. He lacked the courage to end his own life, but he could help those who were in the same hell he was enduring.

He had exchanged pleasantries with other members of the congregation, shaken many hands and then he found his horse and galloped home. His head was pounding, the pain affecting his sight, making the road ahead a blur. When he arrived at his home, he rushed into the house, startling his servants and locked himself in his study. Half an hour later he left.

***

SIR SAMUEL NEEDED to remove himself from Bridgwater. The ignominy of a suicide's burial would have to take place elsewhere.

As he pondered the question of a suitable location, he remembered climbing to the top of Glastonbury Tor with his father and brothers. When they reached the top, they had sat for a while to enjoy the scenery. They could see a colourful patchwork of fields below them and the sun was lighting up the Bristol channel in the distance. His father, looking up at the ruined church told them the story of Abbott Whiting of Glastonbury. As small boys they had delighted in the horror of it. He could still remember the revulsion he felt. He imagined he could hear his father's voice.

"Richard Whiting was a distant relation on my mother's side. Now you know from your history lessons that Cardinal Thomas Wolsey had obtained permission from King Henry VIII to confirm Richard Whiting as the Abbot of Glastonbury. The abbey was one of the most influential in England and one of the richest. Close on one hundred monks lived in the monastery and the sons of the gentry and nobility were educated there before going on to university." A family had seated themselves close to them, interested in his father's story. His father acknowledged them and continued.

"Richard Whiting was held in high esteem. The first ten years of his management were peaceful and prosperous. In 1534, Whiting signed his assent to the Act of Supremacy. Whiting was assured that Glastonbury Abbey was safe from dissolution.

In 1535 the Suppression of Religious Houses Act had brought about the dissolution of small monasteries. By 1539 Glastonbury was the only monastery left in Somerset. Abbot Whiting refused to surrender the Abbey and was sent to the Tower of London where he was examined by Thomas Cromwell and then was sent to Wells, where a trial took place and he was convicted of treason for remaining loyal to Rome.

He was taken to Glastonbury with two of his monks. They were all fastened on hurdles which were dragged by horses to the top of Glastonbury Tor where they were hung, drawn and quartered. Abbot Whiting's head was fastened over the west gate of the deserted Glastonbury Abbey and his limbs were displayed at Bridgwater, Wells, Bath and Ilchester."

"Yuk!" Samuel could remember his youngest brother getting his legs smacked for the remark. He smiled to himself, his little brother had said what he and his other brothers were thinking. He had stared fearfully at the ruin and had been glad to scamper back down the hill and run to the carriage that was waiting to take them home to supper.

***

It was appropriate, Sir Samuel decided. His confused brain saw the martyrdom of his distant relative as a sign. He was desperate to reach Glastonbury before nightfall and spurred his horse on. As he passed the church of St Mary The Virgin in Westonzoyland he remembered the horror of what happen on 7 July 1685, the day when he had lost his beloved Henrietta. His horse was tiring. The poor animal exhausted by the fast gallop. His master was a considerate rider, but now there was an unusual cruelty in his demand for more speed. The horse faltered; the animal nearly tripped on the uneven ground. Sir Samuel realised that he should allow his mount to have a short rest. He pulled the horse to a standstill, dismounted and led him to a stream. The water was clear and cool, the bubbling sound as it danced over some rocks was soothing.

As Sir Samuel let the horse drink he thought about his sons and daughter. They had been so quick to send him to the hospital in Bath when his melancholy had overtaken him. He had resented the way they had made him someone else's problem. He understood now. He had been selfish. They had lost their brother and mother. He, of all people, the widower who had struggled to forgive his wife for leaving him to grieve alone should have been strong enough to support them as a proper father should. He had done nothing for them, never once tried to find out how they felt. The sun was sinking, and it would soon be dark, he must press on. He knew what he must do.

A horseman approached and called a greeting, jolting Sir Samuel from his sombre thoughts. He was suddenly aware of Glastonbury Tor looming in the distance. The tower of the ruined church of St Michael standing defiant, waiting for him to make amends.

***

WILLIAM HAD SPURRED his horse to a gallop and both rider and horse arrived breathless at the vicarage. He dismounted and hastened to the front door. It opened; the maid had heard his arrival.

"I need to see your master urgently." Hugh had been in the hallway and had recognised William's voice.

"William, what brings you here? You sound agitated."

"We must talk, somewhere private."

"My study, Angela, some wine to my study please. William, this way."

William had often been in Hugh's pleasant study. There was a strong smell of pipe tobacco hanging in the air. One wall had a bookcase and the other walls had watercolours painted by Barbara. William admired the latest painting of Jane and Anne. A large black cat occupied one of the aging but comfortable chairs. Hugh clapped his hands together.

"Move, Katie move." Katie gave an indignant meow as she scurried out of the room and nearly tripped up Angela who was carrying a tray of drinks. She set it down and quickly retreated.

"So, William, you are obviously upset. What has happened?"

"It is difficult for me to begin." William took a sip of wine. "The recent deaths, the suspected murders." William hesitated. "I have been told who is responsible."

Hugh lent forward, and nearly knocked his wine off the table. 'Who is it?"

"Get ready for a shock Hugh. It's Sir Samuel."

"Are you mad! Whatever makes you think it's Sir Samuel?"

"I saw Percy Collins at the reception after the coronation. He had travelled from the Isles of Scilly in attendance to Lord Harcombe. He told me he had seen Sir Samuel drop Molly Fisher's body into the Parrett on the day of the fair."

"My God." Hugh was pacing the up and down. "This is a shocking accusation. Why has it only come to light now?"

"Percy was troubled when he told me, he knew he should have come forward earlier and not protected a murderer. After the incident things were never the same between master and servant; he suspected Sir Samuel might have seen him on the riverbank. Percy's family have served the Gilberts for generations. Loyalty to the family was in his blood. He agonised for weeks, waiting for the body to be found. Wanting to clear his conscience but came to the conclusion that no one would believe him.

Several weeks passed, then out of the blue Sir Samuel came up with the suggestion that Percy should move to the Isles of Scilly for the sake of his daughter's health. Percy's wife was delighted, Percy was relieved, he was uncomfortable working for Sir Samuel knowing what he had seen. Even though he was happy in his new position, his conscience tormented him. He wanted to tell someone what he knew, but on the Scilly Isles he was powerless. When he saw me in London, he believed it was an act of God that had brought us together and he passed his burden on to me."

"You sound bitter."

"I am. I have always had the highest regard for Sir Samuel, I knew that I must tell someone what Percy had told me. But there was no proof."

"You are right. It is only the word of a servant against the word of an esteemed and wealthy landowner."

"There is more. My servant Mary also saw a man push a woman in to the Parrett on the day of the fair." Hugh stopped pacing. He looked at William in amazement. "Young Mary? William how long have you known this?"

"She told me tonight. Her English has not been good enough

before. Even now I have not pressed her for a description of the man. She would find it too difficult."

"So, we have a servant living on the Isle of Scilly and an African woman with little English as our only witnesses." Hugh hesitated. "Sir Samuel acted in an extremely strange fashion after Arthur had graduated. He put enormous pressure on the boy to take up the post in Barbados. I had told Sir Samuel in conversation some time before that Arthur had shown interest in seeing the plight of the slaves at first hand, but he really did push Arthur. Barbara and I and of course the girls were most upset. I now wonder if there was a reason Sir Samuel wanted Arthur settled far away."

"But why would he want Arthur out of the way?" William was frowning

"I don't know. My dear friend, I need to pray. Will you come with me?"

***

THERE WAS A hostelry near the bottom of the Tor. Sir Samuel slowed his horse to a trot. He dismounted and waved to a young lad standing in the yard. Some large raindrops spattered the ground at his feet.

"Boy, fetch me a tankard of ale, and water and oats for my mount" He tossed some coins in the boy's direction. The boy bent to pick them up, then hurried into the pub. A short while later he returned with ale for Sir Samuel, and water and oats for the horse.

"He's hungry." The boy was watching the horse gobble down the oats.

"I rode him too hard." Sir Samuel looked regretful.

"What's his name?" The horse had stopped eating and had nuzzled up to the boy.

"Atlas, boy, I'm going to climb to the top of the Tor. I want to see the sunset. Can you look after Atlas for me?" The boy nodded agreement. Sir Samuel strode off into the pub. It was crowded and noisy. He pushed his way to the bar. A pleasant looking man asked him for his order.

"Are you the landlord?" The man said he was. "A pint of your best ale and I would be obliged if you could provide me with pen and paper." The landlord wiped his hands and disappeared behind the bar. He returned a few moments later with paper, pen and ink. Sir Samuel moved to a table, sat down, downed most of his drink, and then spent a couple of minutes writing.

"The boy outside."

"My son."

"He has a way with horses."

"Aye sir, that he has."

"You can read?"

"Yes sir."

"Keep this note, open it in an hour's time."

As Sir Samuel walked the short distance to the base of the Tor, he smiled at what he knew would be the reaction of the landlord's son when he found that he was the owner of such a splendid mount. He then started the steep ascent, passing the grazing sheep as he tried to ignore the increasingly heavy drops of rain. To his dismay, he realised there were other people climbing up, stoically coping with the slippery path, determined to make their way to the top to enjoy the view of the sun setting over Somerset. He panicked; other people were not part of his plan. He would have to wait until he was alone.

The setting of the sun was spectacular, despite the heavy rain. As it made its descent into the horizon it illuminated the colourful patchwork of fields surrounding the Tor. Sir Samuel had walked around the base of the now derelict church of St Michael. The heavy rainfall came to his assistance as concern about the impending storm hastened the departure of the other visitors. He waited patiently, seeing them gradually disappear into the darkness as they made their descent. Their voices became weaker, then he could hear them no more. There was a loud clap of thunder, followed by a spectacular bolt of lightning. The rain was hammering down. That's good, he thought, it would wash away the blood. The time had come for him to join Abbott Whiting and his monks, he knelt, put his pistol to his head and pulled the trigger.

THE VICARAGE

"I HAVE A christening to officiate. I feel that time is of the essence, William I'm sorry but I think you must ride to the Gilbert estate and engage Sir Samuel in …. something, some county matters, perhaps. I will ride to join you as soon as I am free. You must keep him in his home. You can tell him I am coming to discuss an important matter. I have to prepare. I'm sorry Hugh." Hugh was flustered, he had heard a carriage arrive, he recognised the voice of the baby's father shouting to the coachman.

"I understand Hugh. I will see you later." William whistled to his horse Moonlight. She pricked up her ears and trotted obediently towards her master, William realised that in his haste he had failed to tie her up.

"Come on girl. We have an important job to do." He set off with a heavy heart towards the Gilbert estate.

***

All day heavy clouds had hung overhead. Now as William urged Moonlight to a canter large drops of rain were falling. By the time he reached Gilbert Manor he was soaked. He rang the bell and the door was answered almost immediately. Percy Collin's successor, a pleasant young man with a Bristol accent ushered William into the hall. It seemed to William that the entire household staff was assembled.

"Mr Barham, we are so pleased you are here. We didn't know what to do."

"It's Maurice, I think." The young man nodded.

"Maurice, help me out of my coat, the heavy rain has started to seep through." Maurice looked apologetic.

"I'm so sorry sir, I should have noticed. Ethel, bring a towel for Mr Barham. Please, come into the drawing room, there is a large fire."

With gratitude, William relinquished his heavy riding coat, accepted a towel from Ethel and followed Maurice into the warm, comfortable room. He headed straight for the fireplace and warmed his hands close to the flames.

"That's better, thank you Maurice." Maurice had handed William a large glass of red wine.

"I am here to see Sir Samuel."

"He is not here." Maurice looked uncomfortable.

"I sensed when I arrived that something is amiss in the house."

"You are correct, Sir. My master left the house many hours ago. He had arrived home this morning in a distressed state. He locked himself in his study. When he came out, he pushed passed me without giving me any instructions and hurried out of the house, mounted his horse and galloped off. Sometime later I entered his study and found a letter addressed to Rev. Staunton. Here it is." Maurice pulled the letter from his pocket. William accepted the letter, noted the Gilbert stamp on the sealing wax and quickly downed the last of the wine. He was reluctant to face the heavy rain again but felt he had no choice.

The storm had intensified unsettling Moonlight as William led her carefully along the rain-soaked lane. Thunder raged about them. The storm was coming in from the west, if it continued with the same ferocity it would cause the levels to flood. Maurice had lent William a cape to wear over his coat, it had initially been useful but was now soaked and heavy. He felt enormous relief when he arrived back at the vicarage. Barbara Staunton opened the door to him.

"William, you are soaked, quickly, come inside. Here, I will help you with your wet clothing. Hugh and Dr Macey are in the drawing room."

Hugh had heard William's voice and met him in the hall. "Come, quickly. I have pushed a chair close to the fire, you look cold."

"I am cold Hugh." He turned to Dr Macey. "Doctor, good day to you." William held out his hand and received the warm hand of Dr Macey, who grimaced at William's icy handshake.

"Hugh has told me, William. I am deeply concerned. If what we suspect is true, then I feel that I am in part to blame." William looked as if he was going to object. Dr Macey raised a hand to stop him. "I knew he was ill. I arranged his stay at the hospital in Bath. I was careless not to have noticed that his mental state was still far from normal when he returned."

"You are not an expert in such matters. It is the doctors in Bath who were at fault."

"It's kind of you to say that, Hugh but I disagree, I was negligent in my care of Sir Samuel."

"I agree with Hugh; it was the doctors in Bath who were negligent. I have a letter addressed to you." William passed the letter to Hugh who ripped it open. He bent his head to read, then, after a minute raised his head. He looked tired, depressed, sad.

"It's true. Sir Samuel killed Mabel, James, Molly and Jenny and a woman who was a patient in the hospital in Bath." He waved the letter. "It's a confession. He writes that he intends to kill himself. He is ill. We must find him."

It rained all the next day, and the day after. The countryside to the east of Bridgwater was turned into a lake as the Parrett burst its banks. The town's people walked or rode to the edge of the town to view the flood. A light breeze teased the water into waves, giving the flooded meadows the appearance of an ocean. Those who knew from past experience told all who would listen that it would be weeks before the water would sink away. William and Hugh despaired; pursuit of Sir Samuel was impossible.

BARBADOS, JUNE 1689

"I MUST RETURN. I cannot risk a letter. All correspondence from a prison island can be opened by the authorities." Felicity and Arthur were on the beach, oblivious to the sparking blue sea and golden sand. They had serious matters to discuss.

"I wish I could help my friends. They are all desperate to escape. None of them are safe from the Akwamu."

"Samuel Standerwick has suggested to my sister that she sells them all to Lord Plunkett-Browne. However, I have persuaded her that they will still be in danger as the Akwamu are resourceful and will find a way to get to them. So, I have had a better idea. I will buy them."

"What!" Arthur looked at Felicity in amazement.

"I'll get a good price for them in England. The twins, so handsome, they will fetch a tidy sum as will John, again very good to look at and educated. A brown skinned man with an Irish accent. The society ladies will be fighting over him."

"And George and Thomas?"

"Well, I will give them their freedom. I'm a Protestant; I was on Monmouth's side. George and Thomas deserve their freedom. My brother-in-law has an agent who assists him with the sale and purchase of slaves. I will ask Agatha for her help in contacting him. Having spent money, I will need to capitalise on my venture. She will understand, in fact she will approve of my enterprise." Arthur was looking at Felicity in a strange fashion. "Arthur, what are you thinking?"

"I think your idea is inventive, a clever solution to their problem, but they are men Felicity not a commodity."

"Oh Arthur, really." Felicity turned away. She walked several paces and fumbled in her pocket for a handkerchief.

"Felicity what's wrong? You're crying." When Felicity turned to face him, he could see tears in her eyes.

Felicity dabbed her eyes with a handkerchief. "How can you believe that I would sell the twins and John? It was a joke and you believed me!" Felicity continued to walk away from Arthur.

"Felicity come back." Arthur followed her. "Stop, please Felicity, I'm sorry. I'm not myself at the moment. My suspicions of a man who I have always regarded with admiration and respect have turned me into a mean minded individual. Please, don't run away from me." Felicity stopped and turned to face Arthur

"I think you are the kindest, sweetest person I have ever met." Arthur's voice was shaking.

Felicity studied Arthur for several seconds. "Arthur, I am sorry, but I feel insulted that you would even for a minute suspect me of wanting to gain financial advantage by selling our friends or any man."

"You are right to be angry. Forgive me." Arthur looked so devastated that Felicity, despite herself, smiled.

"Don't look so sad Arthur, I accept your explanation. I do understand that your mind must be in turmoil and I have tried very hard to understand why you feel you have to speak to your father face to face. Have you approached my sister yet? She will not be happy that you are breaking your contract."

Arthur reached out and caught hold of Felicity's hand. He pulled her towards him and hugged her.

"Bless you Felicity for forgiving me, I know you are not happy about my decision. Today I am going to ride to Lord Plunkett-Browne's plantation. I am going to make myself known to his doctor. Lord Plunkett-Browne told me his doctor has trained a young convict to be his assistant. My intention is to ask him if he thinks it is feasible for him and his assistant to cover the medical needs of both plantations for the time I will be away." He noticed that Felicity was frowning.

"You would need my sister's and Lord Plunkett-Browne's agreement as well. You must be aware Arthur that they might not agree."

"I know that. But if the doctor supports my request, then I will approach his and my employer. I intend to tell them that there is a pressing family problem necessitating my return."

"What family problem?"

"I haven't decided yet."

"Say your sister is getting married. They will understand that, as the only brother, it is expected that you attend your sister's wedding."

"Who travels 6,000 miles to a wedding?"

"It's your sister. Surely you would want to be there. Your parents would expect it."

"Felicity, you are right, my parents would." Arthur started to laugh. "You don't know my little sisters; pests both of them. Always trying to find a way to annoy me. I would feel sorry for any man who took them on. I can't believe your sister and his lordship would agree. It seems a bit of a weak reason."

"Not to high society. Believe me. They will think it is a good reason."

"I don't feel comfortable lying."

"Arthur, you have told me that you are convinced that Sir Samuel is responsible for the recent deaths in Bridgwater. You have told me repeatedly that you have no choice, that you have to return, that you fear more deaths."

"I do fear more deaths. If you think my sister's wedding is a good enough reason for leaving my employment, then that is the reason I will give. What will I say to my friends? I can't say my sister is getting married. They will find it odd when they find there is no wedding."

"Just say you have a serious family matter to discuss with your father."

"Um, perhaps." Arthur hesitated. "Felicity excuse me for asking, and please don't take offence again, but if you are not intending to sell John and the others, how can you afford to buy them?"

"Arthur, I am extremely fortunate, I'm wealthy. More so than my sister. My godfather was Lord Christopher Kent. He and his wife had five children, three of whom died in infancy. Their two surviving sons died. One at the battle of Solebay, he was on the Royal James." Felicity hesitated, remembering the sad day her family heard the news.

"Solebay, I know of it because my father had a cousin who survived the battle. It's so sad to hear of a man who died in that indecisive skirmish." Arthur looked solemn.

"Yes, I remember the conversation between my parents, I didn't know Edward, but they did. Losing Edward was a cruel blow for Sir Christopher and his wife because a few months earlier they had lost their other son to smallpox. I am Lord Christopher's heir. He was a good man, a philanthropic man.

He would approve of how I'm spending his money. By helping your friends, I feel I am honouring his memory."

"I think what you have just told me explains a great deal about you." Arthur was looking fondly at Felicity. "You are so nice, for a young woman from a wealthy family you have so much interest in others less fortunate. I met the sisters of some of my chums at Oxford, they were totally immersed in themselves. Felicity!" Arthur realised that tears had again formed in Felicity's eyes. "Don't get upset, why are you upset?"

"Arthur, what you have just said is the nicest thing anyone has ever said to me." Arthur put his arms around her and held her close to him. He felt her heart beating, he kissed her, a long, lingering kiss, and wondered at the wisdom of leaving her.

BARHAM MANOR

"THREE WEEKS, it's been three weeks. It will be impossible to find Sir Samuel. He must be dead by now." William was pacing up and down the room. Sarah looked up from her embroidery.

"I still can't believe it. Sir Samuel a murderer."

"Dr Macey stated with deep conviction that Sir Samuel was unwell. He should have never been allowed to leave the hospital."

"You said that in his letter of confession that he believed his actions were merciful."

"Yes, it was a confused letter. But he wrote that he was in a living hell after the death of his son and Henrietta. He had wanted to die; but had lacked the courage to take his own life. He felt it was his duty to help others similarly bereaved. He now knows that he was wrong, and he is determined to kill himself."

"Poor man. It seems Dr Macey is correct in his diagnosis. William…" Sarah hesitated, she looked uncomfortable. "With what we know the last thing I want to do is organise a celebration."

"A celebration, what is there to celebrate?"

"The atmosphere in town has been so miserable the last few weeks, I thought we should have a celebration of the waters subsiding. Tables in the town square, with music and dancing. What do you think?"

"Sarah, I agree that the town needs something to cheer it up but with so many young men missing the farms need every man available to be working flat out. Perhaps a party for the children."

"I'm sorry William, I wasn't thinking. That's a really good idea."

"I will have to leave all the preparations to you. Mary will be able to help you." William stood up. "I can hear a horse." He walked to the window. "It's Hugh. I will leave you in peace." William left the room and opened the door to Hugh himself, he ushered him into his study.

"A glass of wine, Hugh? You don't look well. Do you have bad news?"

"Unfortunately, I have no news for you. I thought that when the water subsided, we would receive information regarding Sir Samuel, but there has been nothing. Yes, wine please." Hugh gratefully accepted the wine. He paused to take a deep draught.

"We need to tell his family he is missing. We also need to tell them what we know. They have to see his confession." William was pacing up and down.

"Not his daughter. Surely Marjory must be spared the truth about her father?"

"I suggest we approach Alfred Gilbert; he is now head of the family. It will be his decision Hugh."

"He will become Sir Alfred, I suppose. How does it work if the body isn't found?"

"I think a certain length of time has to elapse. I feel that we can safely presume that Sir Samuel has taken his own life." William stopped pacing and sat down. He looked tired.

"His letter makes it clear that was his intention." Hugh finished the glass of wine. "What a terrible time we have had lately. So many lives lost. Now Sir Samuel, a once great man disgraced."

"I will always remember the man he was before he became ill, he was a kind and philanthropic gentleman. I will ride to Gloucester and inform Alfred of what has occurred. The matter can wait no longer."

BARBADOS

THE EXCITEMENT IN the air was tangible. "We have always been impressed by the way you have taken the trouble to call us by our African names. Now, please call us Abraham and Matthew. If we are going to live in England, we must get used to our English names.

"So, which one is Abraham and which one of you is Matthew?"

"I am Abraham, he is Matthew." Both twins had big grins on their faces. They liked being twins and confusing people. "All of us going to England. Thanks to Miss Loveridge."

"I'm coming back, but I will make sure you are all happily established before I return. We have been lucky; Felicity is an angel." Arthur's statement bought knowing smiles from the twins.

The next piece of luck was that there was a British Navy sloop patrolling the Caribbean Sea on a Show-the-Flag mission. It was in Caribbean waters to remind the Spanish, French and Dutch of the British presence in the islands. In a week's time the sloop would be returning to England and Arthur and his friends would be on board. The men who had been slaves were now all free men. They had the documentation signed by the Honourable Felicity Loveridge to prove it.

Arthur still couldn't believe just how fortunate they had been. Lord Plunkett-Browne had agreed to sharing his doctor, Dr Caswell with the Eastmount Estate. He had been assured by Dr Caswell that his assistant was more than capable with dealing with minor medical problems, and he would be pleased to cover any more serious matters. In fact, Dr Caswell welcomed the opportunity for his assistant to gain more experience. Lady Agatha had also agreed to allow his visit home, she had approved of his desire to attend his sister's wedding.

***

"WE SAIL ON tomorrow's tide. I trust Felicity that you will be a good girl while I'm gone."

"Well..... Lord Horace has told me that his nephew will be arriving soon."

"Lord Horace?"

"Lord Horace Plunkett-Browne. My sister is dropping hints that the nephew and I would make a good match."

"Great, I'm about to sail away and not return for perhaps six months and you are getting excited about the possibility of a suitable husband arriving on the island."

"Arthur when will you ever learn to recognise that I am teasing you. The Plunkett-Browne nephew is guaranteed to be a snobbish bore, the reason I like you so much is because you are a real man, most of the men of my class are just playboys."

"You know that is not fair. So many of the great military and seafaring men come from your class. He could be a wonderful young man."

"Well, if he is, I doubt that he would still be single. Wonderful young men tend to be snapped up quickly."

"Felicity, will you please be serious for a moment." Arthur took Felicity by the hand and led her to a bench. They both sat down.

"I think you know how I feel about you." Felicity didn't speak, she just nodded. "I don't have much to offer you. You are a beautiful, wealthy young woman."

"Stop Arthur. Just stop. Please don't say any more about my wealth." She surprised Arthur by leaning forward and kissing him. "I promise I will still be here when you return. And I will still be single. We will have another serious talk then."

***

HMS LADY CORNWALL was a tidy looking vessel. She was 50 feet in length, weighed 65 tons and carried six guns. Her captain, James Oliver was near retirement. The Show-The-Flag mission was a pleasant task for a man who had spent much of his naval career in conflict with the Dutch.

After a tearful farewell from Felicity, Arthur and his friends boarded the sloop. Barbados was John's place of birth, the only home he knew. Abraham and Matthew had vague memories of life in Africa, but since the age of 10, the island had been home for them. Thomas and George were relieved to be free men again. All the young men were silent, deep in thought as the crew went about their duties and the ship slipped anchor and set out for England.

The Lady Cornwall was a well-equipped and comfortable vessel. On the first night of the return voyage the guests were invited to join the captain and his officers in his cabin which was surprisingly spacious. Candles flickered in the light breeze entering the cabin through the open ports. It was a calm night; the ship was rolling gently.

The food and wine were excellent. Arthur was astonished by how well the twins and John conducted themselves. They were now free men, but Arthur had expected them to take some time to recognise that fact. There was nothing servile about the handsome young men engaged in conversation with the naval officers. Their experience of the outside world was negligible, and they gave the seamen a welcome opportunity to boast of their knowledge of countries they had visited. The twins had been introduced as accountants who worked for Sir Robert Eastmount who were travelling to Bristol to finalise some business matters. John was introduced as Sir Robert's surveyor, travelling to London to recruit an assistant.

In the morning, to their surprise, a hearty breakfast of bacon and eggs was served up. When they were taken on a tour of the ship, they found the source of the eggs. The cook, Cadoc, a rotund gentleman with a lilting Welsh accent explained that Captain Oliver always had half a dozen hens on board.

"The crew will have bread and porridge for their breakfast, and a jug of beer. We took on supplies in Jamestown, but they won't stay fresh for long. The meals for the first couple of days will be the best while I have fresh produce to work with. Then I have to use preserved ingredients. I have salted ham and lamb. Salted fish, mostly herrings and dried vegetables, dried apples and prunes. I make bread fresh every day, only problem is the weevils, they get into the bags of flour. Nasty little creatures they are." Cadoc shook his head. "We are well stocked; captain always buys plenty. You never know when you might be becalmed. Nothing worse than a hungry crew."

"I learnt last night that we have a 6,000 miles journey ahead of us." John sounded rather worried.

"That's correct. We just have to hope that the weather is kind to us. Cuts up really rough sometimes." Cadoc led them the upper deck. "It's going to be a fine day. I'm going to have half an hour in the fresh air before I have to start preparing the lunches."

"Cadoc, thank you for showing us around." John spoke for the others. "The first lieutenant invited us to spend some time on the quarterdeck. Enjoy your rest." Cadoc was already making himself comfortable well out of the sun.

BARHAM MANOR

PAUL KNOCKED ON the door of his father's study. His knock was responded to with a gruff "Come in."

"Father, are you busy?"

"Well, I was reading through some documents, but I always have time for you son. You look troubled, what's the matter?"

"Charles Heathfield says that it's good that his uncle in Bristol is a slaver. He says his uncle is really, really rich and uses some of the wealth he gets from transporting slaves to help the poor in Bristol. He is having a school built."

"That's very worthy of him, but if you are really really rich, it is easy to be generous."

"Charles says his uncle told him the slave trade is important to the economy. We have a shipping business. Uncle Clive and Auntie Lucinda's house is so much bigger than ours, if the slave trade is a good thing, why aren't we part of it?"

"Would you really be happy to be rich knowing that your wealth came from the destruction of the lives of others? Many Bristol merchants are but I would not want to be them. Paul, I'm disappointed in you. I know there are many who believe that the slave trade is good for Britain. Merchants and planters warn that abolition would mean the whole economy of Britain would collapse."

"Charles says that Africans enslave each other."

"I believe that is true. I have read that there are frequent disputes between the many different tribes. Prisoners are enslaved or even executed by other Africans. I have heard an argument that Britain is in fact saving some Africans from certain death by removing them from their enemies..... just a moment Paul I can I heard voices in the hall. I'm expecting a letter from Bristol." The door opened and Mary came in and handed William a letter.

"Now where were we? Ah yes; another argument for slavery is that Africans are unskilled, uneducated savages. Which, Paul is not true. Think of Mary. She managed to learn English. I know that there is no way I could learn an African language.

I was reading an article about the cruelty of the slave trade only today. Now where did I put the newssheet?" William stood up and crossed to a small table by the side of an easy chair. "Here it is. I suggest you read the article; it describes the whole process. Here, make yourself comfortable."

Paul looked tiny sitting in a grown-up armchair. He raised the paper to his eyes and read for several minutes.

Paul put the newssheet down, he looked upset. "It's horrible. Slaves are human beings, but they are treated like animals. Would Mary have been treated like that?"

"I'm sure she was. When her English is better, she will be able to tell us."

"William, I could hear what you were saying from the hall. Paul is too young to learn of such things!" Sarah had burst into the room in an agitated state.

"No mother, I'm not. I know there are boys my age who are slaves. I have seen them in Bristol. Thank you, father for not treating me like a child. I know what I am going to say to Charles tomorrow."

ABOARD THE LADY CORNWALL

THE HENS STARTED to make soft peeping and trilling noises. One of the older hands saw that Arthur was puzzled. "A storm's coming." He explained. Arthur, bending low to avoid hitting his head, made his way up from a lower deck to fresh air.

He was greeted by the sight of a dark, turbulent sea. Black clouds filled the sky, and he was nearly knocked off his feet by the force of the wind. There was frantic activity all around, the hands were hard at work. They all knew their duties. The shrill sound of pipes signalling orders and the howling of the wind was exhilarating. Arthur felt a tap on his shoulder, it was John.

"Thrilling isn't it." Said Arthur.

"Thrilling maybe Arthur, but I don't think you understand how dangerous a storm at sea can be. Look at those poor sods climbing the rigging. I couldn't do it. I would be so terrified I wouldn't be able to move."

"It's getting worse". Interjected George who with Thomas and the twins were now on the upper deck. A sudden gust of wind sent all the men staggering, desperately trying to keep their balance. Whipped by the fierce wind, ferocious waves were beginning to crash over the deck. Arthur, to his horror and em-barrassment realised he was going to be sick and as he vomited the ship tilted to starboard. His friends left him to his misery, realising they could not just stand and watch the valiant efforts of the crew. Waves were now washing over the deck every minute while above them there was a desperate battle to reduce sail. It was man versus wind and wind was winning.

"What can we do?" Thomas was moving forward, holding on to ropes as he progressed slowly towards the bosun.

"You and your friends could hang on to the ropes to help steady the sails as the crew reef them. If you are going to remain on deck, then you must never let go of the ropes, we won't be able to stop and pick you up if you get washed overboard."

The instruction was shouted, but the words were nearly

drowned out by the noise of other shouted orders, the shriek of the wind and turbulent sea. Everyone on deck was soaked to the skin and Arthur, recovered from his sickness, joined his friends in the battle to reduce sail. Theirs was the easy job compared to those working up top, but it was still difficult as the ship constantly rolled heavily to port.

"Still enjoying it Arthur?" John shouted. Arthur shook his head. The next giant wave came close to knocking him into the tempestuous sea as he clung grimly to the safety line.

It being too risky to light a stove in such conditions, that night's meal was just ship's biscuit and water. Nobody cared too much, all on board were exhausted and grateful to have survived. Many men suffered from bruises and cuts; the most serious injury was to a young lad who had broken his arm. Arthur had attached it to a crude splint and promised to do a better job the next day.

THE NEXT MORNING

The storm had abated, they knew the sun must have risen because the darkness of the night had disappeared. In its place was a thick fog, cold and clammy, impeding the light. After the soaking of the previous day all on board felt chilled to the bone. Cadoc was busy working on a hot meal to warm them up. His kitchen had been turned upside down by the storm, but he had seen it all before and tackled the task of getting it ship shape with great gusto. The sound of his splendid baritone voice drifted to the upper decks, ending the eerie silence of the dense fog and making everyone smile.

Captain Oliver and his officers were standing with their glasses to their eyes, anxiously hoping they wouldn't see an approaching vessel. It was as if the Lady Cornwall was travelling in a cloud, with no wind they were drifting aimlessly. There was a sudden exclamation from the captain. Thinking he had seen another vessel, he asked for confirmation from his officers, but they had seen nothing. "If I did see her, then she's close. Keep looking. We could collide."

Arthur and his friends were standing on the upper deck, well back from the navy men. Wanting to know what was going on but not wanting to get in the way.

"I can see her. She's close to starboard, stand by to fend her off!" The second lieutenant shouted. The instruction was given just in time. Looming before them was a brig, everyone held their breath as the two vessels came within a few feet of each other.

"Ahoy there, Captain Oliver of the Lady Cornwall." The captain shouted, hoping his voice would be heard.

"Captain Kemplyn, Robert Blake out of Bridgwater." Came the response. "That was a close shave!"

"Where are you heading?"

"Africa."

Arthur approached Captain Oliver. "Captain, I know the Robert Blake's owner. There is no way she would be sailing for Africa. Something's wrong."

There was a break in the fog and all on board the Lady Cornwall could see Africans standing on the quarterdeck of the Robert Blake. Two were holding guns.

The twins began to talk to each other in their African tongue. Abraham called out something to the Africans on the quarterdeck. An animated exchange took place.

Abraham turned to Captain Oliver "We want to go on board. The ship is in the hands of the slaves. They are using the crew to sail the boat to Africa and say they will then release the crew and the ship."

"Abraham find out how the Robert Blake came to be used as a

slaver. I know the owner, he abhors slavery."

"I think there is much we need to find out." He and Matthew were preparing for the transfer. A stout rope had been attached to the mast and the twins were going to swing themselves across the narrow gap between the ships. There was now an absolute calm and neither ship was moving.

***

IT WAS AT LEAST an hour before the twins indicated that they wanted to return. The calm sea had allowed the two ships to remain close together and the twins made the crossing back without any difficulty. Arthur and his friends had to wait to find out what the twins had to report because Captain Oliver insisted on speaking to them first.

"I think it best you make your report to me in my cabin." The twins looked at their friends apologetically, acknowledging their frustration. They dutifully followed the captain.

The two ships were still becalmed. The fog was gradually lifting. After what seemed like an hour, but was in fact only 15 minutes, Captain Oliver returned to the deck. "Matthew and Abraham are waiting for you in my cabin." Their friends looked surprised, "Hurry, if the wind picks up, we will drift away from the Robert Blake."

The four men moved quickly to the lower deck where they entered the gloom of the captain's cabin. Candles flickered illuminating wooden bookcases and leather-bound chairs in which Matthew and Abraham were sitting. They stood up when their friends arrived.

"Captain Oliver was mysterious – what is it you have to tell us?" Arthur was looking concerned.

"We have found out from Captain Kemplyn that the Robert Blake was lent to the Pemberton-Harvey Trading Company. He knows that the owner William Barham would never have allowed one of his ships to be used for the slave trade. To Captain Kemplyn's horror, when he arrived at Bristol he was instructed to sail to Africa and pick up a consignment of slaves. He could not refuse, even though he hated what he had been ordered to do.

He and his crew had no knowledge of how to transport slaves. They had no stomach for cruelty to defenceless men, women and children and were lax in their control of them. The result was that the slaves easily took over control of the ship. He said no one was hurt. He and his crew are to sail back to the African coast where the slaves know an area where they believe they will be safe. Then Captain Kemplyn and his crew hope they will be allowed to sail back to Bridgwater. Matthew hesitated. He looked at his brother. "We are going to sail back to Africa with them."

There were gasps from the others.

"We will miss you all." It was Abraham who spoke, concerned by the shocked expressions on his friends' faces. "Please understand we want to go. Also, we will be useful. We can translate for the captain and crew. Before our arrival, they have been communicating with hand signals and pointing at maps. We have already been of service to Captain Kemplyn. He and his crew no longer feel in danger from the slaves. They had naturally been nervous but have been promised that they will be freed and allowed to sail back home."

"Are you sure, don't make a hasty decision." Arthur was worried.

"We were so relieved to be away from the plantation and have our freedom, we would have settled anywhere in the world. But now, now we have the opportunity to see our home again and help our people. We will miss you all, but we have to go." Matthew felt his brother pull on his arm.

"Katlego, we have to go now. If the wind comes up transferring to the Robert Blake could become impossible."

"I am shocked. It is difficult to take in all you have told us. In my heart I understand why you are leaving us, but I will miss you." John was distressed.

"If you find that your homeland disappoints you, then you can sail back with the captain and his crew" Captain Oliver cut into what he worried could be long winded farewells. "Matthew, Abraham you must hurry." The twins were already on their feet. They had possessions to pack.

"You are right captain; this may not be goodbye. We must get to our cabin and get our belongings; we will see you on deck in a few minutes." Then they were gone.

John sat down. He put his head in his hands. "It's so sudden, in a few minutes they could be gone from our lives forever."

"They are so excited. I think they are doing what is best for them. Come on lads, our friends need us to look cheerful." George was being positive.

They hastened to the upper deck. The fog had almost dissipated. The sun was breaking through. There was a light wind and the sloop was tossing in the shallow swell. Matthew and Abraham appeared on deck, both with their possessions strapped to their backs. They hugged each of their friends in turn, then shook hands with the captain. They were about to shake hands with the officers and other members of the crew when Captain Oliver intervened. "You must go now! The wind is increasing." Matthew was the first to swing across; he sent the rope back to Abraham who caught it. He fastened it around him, then made the short crossing to the Robert Blake.

The twins stood together on the deck and waved to their friends. Captain Oliver was right, within minutes of the twins completing the crossing the swell had increased and the wind was beginning to tug at the sails that had been reset after the storm. The two boats were straining hard on the ropes linking them. Crews on both boats released the ropes and the wind completed the separation.

The friends stood at the stern and watched the Robert Blake slowly disappear into the distance. She became smaller and smaller and eventually she was gone. They stood for a while, staring at the empty ocean, each of them wondering if they would ever see Matthew and Abraham again.

TURLE FARM, NEAR BRIDGWATER

NANCY TURLE DIDN'T know whether to be happy or sad. She was happy that her boys Tom and Matt had formed a friendship with young Mary, the Barham's servant. What she wasn't so happy about was the worrying realisation that for both boys the relationship had developed beyond friendship.

Mary, with her tall, slim body, enchantingly pretty face and spectacular dark eyes was a delight to behold. Her thick tight curls were worn piled up on her head, usually bound with a red ribbon. Nancy had learnt a new word. Sarah Barham had said Mary was……. what was it she called her? Oh yes, sounded like it began with a X… exotic, that was it. Sarah said Mary was exotic.

Why oh, why did her boys have to fall for her? Mary's English was improving, but she still made funny mistakes. Mistakes that, in the eyes of Tom and Matt made her all the more appealing.

Nancy could see disaster ahead. If Mary fell for one of them, then the other one would be broken hearted. Nancy knew that she was lucky to still have her sons. So many of her friends had lost their boys in the rebellion. Many having suffered terrible deaths, causing their mothers to live in perpetual grief. Nancy would always be grateful to William Barham for saving her boys, but so many times she had wished the Barham's had left Mary with Sarah's sister in Bristol.

Tom and Matt could have their choice of the many pretty single girls in Bridgwater. Good girls who Nancy had known since they were babies. Her friend's daughters. Girls who knew what it was to be a farmer's wife. Before Mary came on the scene, Nancy had her eye on Rachael Maidment for Tom and Harriet Ridley for Matt. Both pretty as a picture, real English roses. Hard working daughters of farming families.

Nancy knew that Mary was a hard-working young woman, but she hadn't been born to get up at the crack of dawn on a bitterly cold frosty morning to tend to the needs of animals. Tom and Matt were always teasing her about wearing a cloak on what they regarded as a hot summer's day. Nancy wondered if eventually Mary would get used to the cold, but she thought it unlikely. She had always thought that Tom and Matt would bring their wives to live at the farm. She would move into a cottage in the town. Now she feared that if Mary chose one of her sons, the other would most likely move away. He would start up somewhere else. It was a prospect that Nancy dreaded.

The young women of Bridgwater were wary of Mary. Quite understandably jealous. So many young men had been killed. So many transported. Many Bridgwater girls had lost their boyfriends. They faced spinsterhood or moving away from Somerset to somewhere with healthy single young men and few single young women. In so many homes in Bridgwater tearful daughters had informed their parents that they were contemplating leaving home.

The fact that two of the most eligible men in town were in thrall of a freed slave was infuriating. It wasn't as if they didn't like Mary. She was difficult not to like, always smiling, always willing to help if she saw someone in difficulty. They all felt sorry for her. They couldn't imagine what it must be like to be captured, dragged away from your home, family and friends and end up in a country where no one spoke your language. Yes, they liked her, they just wished that Mary would go back to whence she came.

The river Parrett was looking its worst, the tide was out but turning and there was just a stream of muddy water flowing upstream from the sea. The muddy banks were exposed, not an attractive sight Nancy thought to herself as she walked towards town. She was suddenly aware of someone behind her calling her name. She turned around and saw it was Temperance Lukins. Nancy stopped and waited for Temperance to catch up with her.

"Great news Nancy, wonderful news. The boys are coming home!" Temperance caught her breath. "I came to the farmhouse to tell you. I guessed that you were walking into town. King William and Queen Mary, they have pardoned the rebels. They can come home. Isn't that wonderful news?"

"Indeed, it is. It's wonderful news. It's the best news I have had since my boys came back to me. Oh, all those families, they will have their boys back as well. Temperance, my dear, are you alright?" Nancy could see the excitement in Temperance's eyes dimming. She now looked close to tears.

"If only my Sam had been transported, then he would be coming home to me." Temperance said in a quiet voice, so quiet Nancy thought she was speaking to herself. Tears started to fill Nancy's eyes as she took her friend into her arms and held her tight. Her worry over her sons dissipated as she comforted the heart broken woman.

ON BOARD THE LADY CORNWALL

"ADMIRAL BLAKE WILL be turning in his grave. A vessel named after him used as a slaver. What do you think?" George was whittling away at a piece of wood.

"Perhaps he would have been pleased that the slaves have commandeered it and are on their way to freedom." Thomas said.

Arthur nodded his head in agreement.

"Who was Admiral Blake?" John asked

"He was a colonel in Cromwell's army. Won the Siege of Bristol, the Siege of Lyme Regis, the Siege of Taunton and the Siege of Dunster." George was counting the victories off on his fingers. "I remember being taught about his triumphs at school."

"And then he became Cromwell's General at Sea. Prince Rupert of the Rhine was trying to stop Cromwell landing in Ireland in an attempt to prevent the Parliamentarians taking Ireland from the Royalists. Blake blockaded Prince Rupert's fleet and Cromwell was able to land in Dublin." Thomas was showing that he too remembered his history lessons. Arthur was the only one aware of John's rising anger.

"Why do you know so much about his man?"

"Well John, he's our local hero. A Bridgwater man."

"Do you have any idea what Cromwell did to Ireland?" John stood up. He started pacing up and down in front of his friends. "You know my father was transported because he rebelled against Cromwell. Your man Blake helped Cromwell to invade Ireland. The result was 50,000 men, woman and children transported, famine and bubonic plague for those left behind. Catholicism banned, and priests executed.

My father came from Wexford. The Parliamentarian army stormed into the town while negotiations for surrender were taking place, 2,000 Irish soldiers were killed and 1,500 innocent townspeople. You are taking me to Bridgwater? You want me to live in a town where the hero is Cromwell's man? I should have joined Matthew and Abraham and sailed for Africa."

There was silence. George and Thomas had forgotten about John's background. They heard footsteps; it was Captain Oliver.

"I overheard your conversation. I hope you don't mind me joining you." The captain was hesitant, sensing a strained atmosphere.

"It's your ship, captain." John managed a smile.

"John, I can understand how you feel, but there was evil on both sides. My mother was born in Ireland. She met my father when he came to Ireland as an officer in the Parliamentarian army. It's quite a love story. Her family were English Protestant settlers who had been the subject of atrocities during the 1641 uprising. The Catholic's slaughtered the Protestants in the most ungodly manner.

Catholics imprisoned Protestants in the church in Portadown County Armagh. They were told they were to be deported back to England. They were marched to the town bridge were Catholics using swords and pikes demanded they strip. They were forced to jump into the river. It was November, most drowned in the icy water; some died of exposure, some were shot, a survivor claimed that 100 men, women and children perished.

In nearby Kilmore English and Scottish men, women and children were burned to death in a cottage where they were imprisoned.

My Protestant grandfather and uncles fought with Cromwell. They were sad to see my mother leave Ireland but pleased she had met a man they admired.

Religion was the reason why some men joined the Parliamentarian army. For them the invasion of Ireland was a religious war. Many of Cromwell's army were Puritans. They regarded Catholics as heretics."

"My apologies, captain." They hadn't realised the second lieutenant was hovering waiting to speak, he looked agitated. "The bosun has urgent need of your orders." The two navy men hurried away.

Arthur had also remembered his history lessons. "We were taught that Cromwell invaded Ireland for several reasons. The English parliament had a long-standing commitment to reconquer Ireland after they lost it in 1641. They were aware that Catholic Royalist troops were preparing to invade England and restore the monarchy. Cromwell had borrowed heavily for the invasion. To repay his debts he had to confiscate land from the Irish landowners and give it to his creditors. We were never taught about the deaths and transportation." Arthur was interrupted by Captain Oliver's return.

"John, I have something in my cabin I would like to show you. I won't be long."

The men were once again silent. The only sound was the creaking of the ship's timbers, the wind whistling through the sails and the occasional shouted order from a ship's officer to the men. The ocean was subdued; John's outburst was still on the minds of his friends. They heard footsteps; Captain Oliver returned.

"I have here a book. It is the rules and regulations of the Navy. Here, take it John."

John took the book and read the title *The Laws of War and Ordinances of the Sea.* The author was Commander at Sea Robert Blake.

"Captain Oliver what is it you are trying to tell me?"

"Robert Blake was a great man, a successful commander of men on land and an outstanding seaman. He commanded the British navy against the Turks. He succeeded in freeing Christian slaves held by Moslems on the Barbary Coast. He supported his men; he was instrumental in raising the pay of seamen.

I fought with him during the war with the Dutch. It was imperative that Britain had control over the English Channel. As a nation we are dependent on overseas trade. Blake defeated the Dutch and kept Britain a dominant world trader, no matter who was on the throne.

Blake's last and greatest victory was against Spain. The British fleet destroyed an entire Spanish squadron of 16 ships. It was a triumph, the result of careful planning, caution and discipline. Blake wrote several books on discipline in the navy. Discipline saves lives. Robert Blake was a man I admire."

"I hear what you say, you might admire him, but I know my father would have hated him." John was still looking unsure.

"I understand your revulsion at discovering a man who did so much for Cromwell is regarded as a hero in the town you were hoping would be a sanctuary for you. My years at sea, fighting battles, seeing good men die for one cause or another has made me more realistic about the nature of conflict. Blake might have been your father's enemy, but he was a good servant to the cause he believed in."

"I agree with Captain Oliver, John. I think I speak for Thomas and George." Arthur looked at Thomas and George and they both nodded their agreement.

"They dug him up." It was George who spoke.

"What do you mean they dug him up?" John was astonished.

"Robert Blake was given a state funeral by Cromwell at Westminster Abbey. When King Charles came to the throne, he had Blake dug up and interred in the church next door."

"The King ordered him to be dug up?" John looked shocked.

"Well John, Robert Blake was Cromwell's man. The King wanted what Robert Blake did for Britain in defeating the Turks, Dutch and the Spanish forgotten. He wanted him written out of history. That's why he is remembered in Bridgwater. Bridgwater won't let him be forgotten."

"Well said Arthur."

"I agree, George. Well said." Thomas clapped Arthur on the back.

BRIDGWATER

SIR SAMUEL HAD been greatly revered in Bridgwater. A major landowner and an extremely wealthy man he had always taken a fatherly interest in the affairs of the town's folk. It was common knowledge that the death of his eldest son at the battle of Sedgemoor, followed by the suicide of his wife had unhinged him. He was never quite the same when he returned from hospital. He looked well, but there was a deep melancholy about him. There was a deep melancholy about so many in the town.

When he suddenly went missing, it was said that he had returned to hospital in Bath. His servants were seen in the town, going about their business as normal. Then it was announced that Sir Samuel had passed away and had been buried in Bath. There was to be a memorial service at St Mary's. Some thought it strange that he was being buried in Bath but said that the ways of the gentry were often strange.

Gilbert Manor was to be put up for sale. The house had always been intended for the eldest son, who had died at Sedgemoor. Sir Gilbert's sons and daughter had forged lives away from Somerset and none of them desired to return to what should have been the home of their brother. "Too many sad memories, think what happened to their brother and Lady Henrietta." The gossips were saying.

No one knew the identity of the man who lay at the crossroads outside Glastonbury. A story about a well-dressed gentleman who climbed the Tor and killed himself at the time of the flood eventually made its way to Bridgwater. There was some speculation as to who the gentleman could have been, but Sir Samuel's name was never mentioned.

BARHAM MANOR

"SARAH, SARAH, WHERE are you?" William had arrived back from the shipyard in an agitated state.

"William, whatever is the matter?" Sarah the entered the hall from the kitchen. "I was just discussing the week's menus with cook."

"Our brother-in-law is the matter. We have had no information as to the whereabouts of the Robert Blake. The ship should have been back in dock by now. I'm going to have to ride to Bristol. Why I have to go I just don't know. Clive should be riding to me to explain the delay. The Robert Blake is needed for the next consignment of rope."

"Oh William, I'm so sorry. I agree, its rude of Clive not to keep you informed. In fact, I'm shocked. Clive is a perfect gentleman, it's not like him to behave in a discourteous manner. William, I think somethings wrong."

"Something is definitely wrong." William rang a small handbell. Mary arrived in the hall. "Mary, please tell Philip to pack my bag. I will be away for two nights." Mary bobbed a curtsey and left.

"You need to calm down, William. You can't start a journey in the state you are in. Come, relax for a while, you must eat before you leave." William turned towards his study and Sarah went back to the kitchen to finish her discussion with cook. When she returned she saw that William hadn't relaxed; he was pacing up and down.

"I thought that Edward might have been given information regarding the ship. Clive knows that we are partners. Edward hoped that I had some information. We are in a mess Sarah. It's not funny. We have a contract to ship the rope and nothing to ship it in. I can't believe Clive would let me down like this."

"I'm really worried, I wish I could come with you."

"It's out of the question, I must move fast. Ah, here's Mary." Mary entered the room with a tray of bread and cheese and a glass of ale. "Thank you, Mary. You spoke to Philip?"

"Yes sir, he will leave your bag in hall." Mary left.

"William, please sit down, eat your meal. I will check that Philip has packed your bag correctly."

BRISTOL, THE HOME OF CLIVE AND LUCINDA PEMBERTON-HARVEY

WILLIAM SENSED AN atmosphere as he was ushered into the drawing room. His sister-in-law Lucinda looked drawn. She stood when William entered the room and rushed towards him and embraced him. William was shocked. Lucinda had never shown such affection for him before. "I'm so very sorry William." She said.

"Lucinda, what have you to be sorry about?" The door opened and Clive entered the room. William's worst fears were realised. Clive's usual military bearing had softened into a hunched shouldered stance. His irritating confidence was absent. He looked destroyed.

"William, good to see you. I can guess why you are here. I have to apologise. It is unforgivable of me to have made you undertake a journey I should have made. It was my place to come to you, but I have been hanging on here hoping for some positive news." Clive held out his hand and William shook it. "Please take a seat William, refreshments will be here in a few minutes."

"Thank you, Clive. I am somewhat perturbed that you failed to have the courtesy to keep me informed as to the whereabouts of the Robert Blake. My partner Edward and I are now in a great deal of difficulty. We have a consignment of rope to ship to Ireland but no vessel to ship it in." The tone of William's voice left his in-laws with no doubt that he was upset.

"Oh, this is terrible, William, we are so sorry." The door

opened. "Ethel is here with the refreshments." Ethel placed the tray on the table and left, ready to report to the rest of the staff that Mr Barham seemed angry. The staff had been speculating for days about the nature of the problem that was causing the master and mistress so much distress.

"William, I have been let down in the most distressing manner. My father." Clive's voice faltered. Lucinda rose from her seat, crossed the room and sat beside her husband. She took his hand. "The truth is my father assured me that the Robert Blake would not be used for the slave trade. He deceived me. I have had three reports that the Robert Blake was seen in Africa loading up with slaves."

"My God Clive. You gave me your word. I abhor the slave trade. Now one of my ships is being used."

"My father has tried to tell me that it was from necessity. We only asked for your help because we had a vessel delayed, then a second ship was late."

"That's no excuse. A promise was broken. Families in Bridgwater, still grieving for the loss of sons at Sedgemoor are now anxiously awaiting news of the crew. Many are Bridgwater men."

"William, there is nothing you can say that will make me feel any worse. I am ashamed. I have resigned from Pemberton-Harvey trading company." William looked surprised.

"What will you do?"

"I am re-joining the army. I never wanted to be part of my father's business. I am ashamed of my father's conduct, but to be perfectly honest with you, my father's dishonesty has given me an excellent reason to leave and let my younger brother take over. Don't say it, William." William looked about to explode. "I know that last thing you want to hear is that your problem has been to my advantage. What can I do? Please tell me. Lucinda and I are mortified by what has occurred."

"I need a ship. You have no news at all as to her whereabouts?"

"It's a mystery. By all the accounts we have received she should be here by now."

"She must have foundered. Those poor souls. Insurance?"

"In due course, but it could be months."

"Get me a ship Clive. I must have a ship."

"Come with me. The Pemberton-Harvey's name is respected. Your contract is to ship to Ireland?" William nodded. "Then I believe we may be lucky. For such a short distance I know a vessel that would be suitable and possibly available."

ON BOARD THE LADY CORNWALL

"BRIDGWATER IS NOT a bit like Barbados, no sparkling blue sea, palm trees, hummingbirds, whistling frogs and turtles but we like it there." The Lady Cornwall was making good progress. A dominant wind filled the sails, the hull was forcing a way through the calm sea. It was satisfying to be skimming across the ocean at speed.

"You forget George that we have the river Parrett."

"Ah yes, the muddy river Parrett. Sometimes it's there, sometimes it's not."

"Thomas, what do you mean, you can't have a river that disappears." John was puzzled.

"Oh, but you can, well most of it anyway. It's tidal. Just like the sea around Barbados. It's just that its more obvious with a river."

"It also has a bore."

"I know you don't mean the river is boring so what do you

mean?"

"A bore is a rush of water. It happens every time the tide comes in but usually it isn't noticeable. A couple of times a year, spring and autumn when there is a flood tide it can be spectacular. The head of the incoming tide forms a large wave that travels up the river against the direction of the current. It travels about six miles an hour. With the passage of the bore the whole appearance of the river changes from a slowly ebbing stream to a turbulent fast flowing river."

"It's quite a sight." George added. The turbulence stirs up all the sediment and the river appears to be a different colour."

"It does sound worth seeing." John did his best to look pleased. "So, what other delights await me in Bridgwater, if I decide to stay in a town where the local hero is Cromwell's man."

"Well." There was a pause, then George spoke up. There are the inns."

"My father told me about inns. Is the ale good in Bridgwater inns?"

"Yes, and so is the cider, that's a brew made from apples."

"What else is there to do in Bridgwater?"

"There's cricket. It's a bat and ball game. It's played in a field between two teams of 11 men each side. In the middle of the field there is an area of 22 yards, 10 feet wide. It's called the pitch. At each end of the pitch there are two short sticks. On top of the sticks there is a piece of wood, called a bail lying across the sticks. Using a stave, that's a wooden stick with a curve at the end, the hitting side player scores runs by hitting a leather ball which is thrown to him underarm by a member of the other team. The batsman can be out if the ball is caught or the ball hits the two pieces of wood and knocks the bail off. When all the men are out the teams swap ends, and it starts all over again."

"You've missed a run out."

"I've left a lot out George. I don't want to confuse John. I just told him the basics."

"I've played cricket. I've been part of the Eastmount team playing against the Plunkett-Browne team. Bongani and Katlego used to play. They were good. Sorry Thomas, but once you started, it would have been rude to stop you. Your face was lit up with the memory of the game. I could see how much you missed playing it."

"We both miss it. I bet you don't know how to play skittles."

"You would win the bet, George." John stifled a yawn, he looked disinterested. If all Bridgwater had to offer was cricket, something called skittles and a muddy river he was thinking he had made a mistake in thinking he could be happy there.

"We haven't told John about the weather."

"George, I know it gets cold. My father told me."

"Just like Ireland, we get a great deal of rain in Somerset. Sometimes we can be cut off from other towns. The land is flat and at times the sea rushes in. People still talk about the flood of 1607. A massive storm caused flooding 14 miles from the coast. People had to climb trees or get on to a roof to survive. Hundreds died and thousands of animals were killed. Then there is snow. Did your father tell you about snow?"

"I know about snow." John was surly. "Are you trying to put me off?"

"No, we want you to settle in Bridgwater. We agree with Arthur. You would make a brilliant teacher. Arthur said the school lost three teachers at the Battle of Sedgemoor. Your mathematical ability is better than that of any of the teachers we had."

"Well, I suppose rain, snow, cold, not much sunshine is paradise compared to chains, cruel overseers, the sound of human misery and despair. I will give it a go. You like it don't you?"

"It's our home." Thomas and George answered in unison, looking towards the horizon and longing for the first sight of England.

BARHAM MANOR

"MOTHER, FATHER, we learnt about Isolda Parewastel." Paul was holding an atlas.

"A most remarkable lady. I am delighted you were told about her extraordinary journey." Sarah was smiling.

"Whose Isolda Pare…. whatever?" Harry had looked up from his book.

"Isolda Parewastel, stupid – and it's none of your business."

"Don't speak to your brother like that." William was irritated. "Whatever are you thinking young man?"

"Well father, Harry wouldn't understand. He wouldn't know how far it is from Bridgwater to Jerusalem. You have to be my age to appreciate that it was an amazing journey for a lady to make in 1361. And it was amazing that, after being tortured by Saracens and left for dead, she escaped and made her way back to Bridgwater. Harry's too young, he wouldn't understand."

Harry stood up and threw his book at Paul. Paul rushed towards his brother and they both fell to the floor. William and Sarah were immediately on their feet, avoiding the flying fists as they tried to separate their sons.

"To bed, both of you!" William shouted.

"We haven't had supper."

"And you won't. Now move. Move!" Both boys hurried from the room.

"Whatever caused them to behave like that Sarah?"

"They are getting older. I have noticed more friction between them recently. Paul regards his little brother as an irritation."

"I will give Paul half an hour to reflect on his behaviour then I will go upstairs and talk to him. We cannot have another display of bad temper from either them, although it was definitely Paul who started the quarrel." William crossed the room to a small walnut table holding a decanter and glasses. "Would you like a glass of wine my dear?"

"I would William, I am still shaken up by the boys' bad behaviour." Sarah accepted the glass handed to her. She studied the deep red liquid before she drank. William returned to his chair.

"I meant to tell you earlier, I saw Mrs Parsons in town today. She looked quite ill. It's the worry over the Robert Blake. I wished I had some news to give her, but I've heard nothing, nothing at all. No sightings. No reports of wreckage."

"Where could she be William?"

"My dear, I just don't know. The terrible fact is that we may never know what became of her. I curse Pemberton-Harvey every day for his trickery."

"William, with the boys behaving so badly I forgot to tell you that I have received a letter from Lucinda. They cannot stay in Bristol. The atmosphere between Clive and his father is toxic. Now that Clive has re-joined the army, and with their boys away at university, Lucinda will often be in the house on her own, except for the servants of course. The hostility between the senior Pemberton-Harvey's and Lucinda and Clive is now affecting Lucinda's social status in Bristol. She is being ostracised by Bristol society."

"Poor Lucinda." William sounded insincere. "I'm sorry Sarah, I know Lucinda is a good kind woman but her inconvenience at being cold-shouldered by Bristol society is nothing compared to the anxiety and suffering of the Bridgwater families who are waiting for news of the Robert Blake."

"I know that, but I am still concerned for my sister. Oh, William I wish she could live closer to us." William crossed the room, he held up the decanter. "Some more wine, my dear?"

Sarah looked at her glass, it was nearly empty. "Yes, I feel this is a night for drinking wine." William refilled both their glasses. He turned to his seat.

"I have a thought; Gilbert Manor is standing empty. I will write to Alfred and inquire as to how the sale of the property is progressing. You must write to Lucinda and ask if she would have any interest in moving to Bridgwater." William put down his glass of wine. "In the meantime, I must have a serious conversation with Paul before I can relax for the evening."

He stood up, smiled at Sarah and left the room.

ABOARD THE ROBERT BLAKE

CAPTAIN KEMPLYN HAD never sailed so far away from England before. He had always longed to sail further than Ireland, Holland, France and Spain, but he had married before he had the opportunity to be captain with a firm of merchant venturers who traded further afield. His beloved wife had not wanted him away from home for long, so he had settled for a steady if unexciting life as master of the Robert Blake. He now thanked God that he had with him two bright lieutenants who were relishing the strange events that now found them heading back to the coast of Africa.

The chance encounter in the fog with the Lady Cornwall and the miraculous addition to the ship's company of Matthew and Abraham had cheered him and his crew. Being able to communicate with the Africans was wonderful. He trusted their leaders; they could have easily thrown him and his crew overboard. They could have killed some of his men just to make him cooperate, but they did not. He had believed all along that they would let the Robert Blake sail back to England but there was just a slight niggle. Could he really trust them? His wife always told him he was too trusting, too ready to see the good in people. Well, Matthew and Abraham with their language ability were obviously useful to the Africans. They had made it clear to the Africans that they would help them only if they guaranteed the ship and crew would be free once the ship reached Africa.

His biggest worry was about his wife. She would be desperate. She would by now have assumed that the ship was lost. That he was dead. He knew that the families of his crew would be mourning their loved ones. There was nothing he could do to ease their anguish. He had written a hasty letter to his wife and given it to Captain Oliver. He had promised that as soon as the Lady Cornwall docked, which could still be weeks away, he would hand it to a messenger with the instructions to make haste with the delivery. The letter would both comfort and alarm his beloved Betty, but there was nothing he could do to change the hand of fate that was sending him so far away from her.

He had also received assurance from Captain Oliver that William Barham would be told of the hijacking of his ship.

EASTMOUNT HOUSE, BARBADOS

FELICITY LOOKED AT herself in the mirror and frowned. She had been irritated when her sister insisted that she should have a new dress for the ball welcoming the Honourable Darius Plunkett-Browne. The dress had been cut in the latest fashion. The neckline was so low that her nipples were close to being on display. Felicity had objected but was told firmly that fashionable young women in London had their dresses cut even lower and their nipples were completely exposed.

She was fully aware that her sister and Lord Plunkett-Browne were trying to match make. She had no interest in meeting Darius. Every day Felicity rode to the dock to see the ships coming in. She knew there was no chance that Arthur would be returning so soon, but it comforted her to imagine the day he would return. She also knew it was too soon for a letter from him. She missed him. She wished she had said more about her love for him when they parted. Her thoughts were interrupted by a knock on the door.

"Miss Felicity; the mistress says please can you hurry. She doesn't want to be late." Felicity opened the door and the maid bobbed a curtsy. "Miss Felicity, you look real fine."

"Thank you Jenny. You don't think it's too low?"

"Oh no Miss, I have heard of the ladies in London. You look just fine."

Felicity hurried down the ornate staircase to find her sister looking magnificent. She was relieved that Agatha had chosen a matronly style that flattered her plump figure and suited her age. The dress was made of blue silk with three quarter length sleeves edged with silver lace. Despite herself, Felicity felt a buzz of excitement. Agatha's obvious delight as she anticipated the evening before them was infectious.

The drive to the Plunkett-Browne mansion was lined with palm trees. Beside each palm tree stood a slave, dressed in the livery of the Plunkett-Browne family.

As each carriage arrived at the house Horace Plunkett-Browne greeted his guests with a small gift. Felicity was amazed to find that her gift was a dainty silver bracelet.

Felicity struggled not to laugh when she noticed Agatha's face when she opened her gift. It was a silver brooch.

"I must say Felicity I have never before attended a function where gifts are given to guests upon arrival. I'm not sure it is in the best of taste."

There was a short reception line of Lord Horace Plunkett-Browne, his wife Lady Iris and his nephew Darius. As Felicity bopped a curtsy to Lady Iris, she was aware that Darius was studying her with great interest. She felt uncomfortable, she rose from her curtsy and extended her hand to the inquisitive young man. She met his eyes. She could see admiration in them. Flustered, she mumbled a few words of greeting. She turned quickly and followed Agatha through to the ballroom.

Felicity had told Arthur that the Plunkett-Browne nephew was guaranteed to be a snobbish bore, a playboy. He might well be, she thought, but he looked like the handsome Prince Charming she had imagined when she was a little girl. She accepted a glass of wine offered by a passing waiter. She alarmed Agatha by drinking all the wine, and then accepting another. Agatha gently took her arm. She guided her through the throng of guests to a seat.

"Darius is a fine-looking young man. I'm sure you will like him."

"He looked at me as if he knew me. I was affronted! Agatha, I'm not stupid, I know you and Lord Horace have hopes that Darius and I might be a match. He is indeed a handsome man, not at all what I expected." Felicity fanned herself, the wine was having an effect. "I fear that you have forgotten I have formed a liaison with Arthur. I am hopeful that when Arthur returns, we may be in a position to make an announcement."

"Arthur is a fine young man, but Felicity, a physician? The son of a clergyman? You must not marry beneath you. Darius has the correct breeding for someone from our illustrious family. He will make the perfect husband for you."

The music for dancing was supplied by a group of musicians formed from Somerset rebels and African slaves. Felicity knew that Lord Plunkett-Browne had gone to the expense of procuring the services of a music teacher from England. He had travelled out with her and Agatha. He had obviously been good at his job because the band played surprisingly well. A waltz had just finished, and the gentlemen were escorting the ladies to their chairs. Felicity was aware that someone had entered the small alcove where she was sitting with Agatha. It was inevitable, Darius was about to ask her to dance.

Felicity studied him. Tall, clearly well-built beneath his pale blue silk jacket. The ruff at the neck of his shirt cradling his handsome face. His wig was parted in the middle, the very latest fashion. She accepted his offer with a bright, tight smile. The first cords of the music announced a minuet, the popular dance from France. It was a formal dance. Felicity had been instructed in the intricate moves before she had left England. She had no doubt that Darius would also be familiar with steps.

Darius guided Felicity into the throng of dancers. Initially, wary of her partner, Felicity's movements had been rigid, then, despite herself, Felicity realised that she was enjoying the dance. Darius was an excellent partner. He had led her expertly through the elaborate routine. The music for another waltz started as they were returning to Agatha. Darius bowed to Felicity. "Would you do me the honour again?" She smiled. "I would be delighted" and she was. Darius swept her into his strong arms and spun her around the ballroom. She felt intoxicated, she knew it was not just the wine she had drunk so rapidly, it was Darius.

ABOARD THE LADY CORNWALL

"LAND AHOY!" At last the call they had been waiting for. England! The wind was whistling through the rigging as the ship rolled on the swell.

"As you are aware Arthur, HMS Cornwall must return directly to London. We will get to London in another two days how long will it take you to get to Bridgwater?"

"With luck five days. It will depend on the fitness of the horses. I will be glad to be on dry land. What will you miss the most about life at sea when you retire?"

"It's been my life since I was 13". Captain Oliver looked thoughtful. He took time to consider his answer.

"The wide-open sea, softly undulating waves, and the horizon in the distance, beckoning, leading to adventure. It must have been wonderful to have been able to discover new lands. As a boy I relished reading about the adventures of Drake, Columbus, Magellan and Vasco da Gama.

I will miss the sea, but I have been looking forward to spending time with my wife and our children. We now have grandchildren and I haven't even seen the latest one. I do hope your family matters can be concluded successfully, Arthur."

"Thank you, captain. You have obviously been happily married."

"I am the most fortunate of men. My wife has endured a great deal being married to a seafaring man."

"I have left the most wonderful woman in Barbados." Arthur was looking distressed. "I should have spoken more convincingly of my intensions, but I hesitated."

"My boy, you look upset."

"It was you talking about your wife and family. I keep worrying that I should perhaps have asked Felicity to marry me. I didn't, I just hinted that I would when I returned to Barbados."

"You say hinted?"

"I'm sure she understood."

"Why did you not make your feelings clear?"

"Felicity is way above my station. I'm just a vicar's son. She comes from a noble family. Also……" Arthur hesitated, he looked miserable. "She is an heiress, captain that's why I hesitated."

"She has shown herself to be fond of you?"

"Most definitely."

"My boy, I think you must complete your family business as quickly as possible and hasten back to Barbados and make your intentions clear. Social standing and money cannot overcome real affection."

"Do you really think that?"

"I do, I have come across several situations where a young woman has fallen for a man who some would regard her social inferior. Young women are good judges of character. You are a fine young man Arthur. Cheer up. You would make any women an excellent husband, and remember absence makes the heart grow fonder."

Arthur stared out to sea. In his mind's eye he could see Felicity standing on the beach, her yellow curls blowing in the wind. Her blue eyes the colour of the sky above her….. and her smile, her delightful smile lighting up her pretty face. It was several moments before he spoke again.

"Thank you for your advice Captain. Whatever happens regarding my problems, returning to England will be a happy occasion for George and Thomas. They will be reunited with their families."

"I must give you the letters now before the excitement of our landing causes me to forget. I have written to the Pemberton-Harvey trading company on Captain Kemplyn's behalf. He had already given me a letter for his wife."

"I can assure you captain that I would have reminded you. I am as anxious as Captain Kemplyn to pass on information regarding the fate of the Robert Blake. Many families in Bridgwater will be desperate for any news."

"I can understand that. I know how my wife has suffered when circumstances have delayed my return. Arthur, what has John decided?"

Arthur laughed, "John has agreed to stay for six months. He has formed a close friendship with George and Thomas. I feel confident that they will do everything they can to make John feel at home in Somerset. If they fail, it will be a great disappointment to me. I feel he has so much he can offer the young lads of Bridgwater. He will make a brilliant teacher. He is such a funny chap, always with a bright smile. I wish I could have had him teach me when I was at school."

"Are you talking about me?" John was suddenly standing behind Arthur.

"I'm only saying good things about you John."

"Captain, I heard the call, 'Land ahoy.' Just how long will it be before we land?"

"It will still be a couple of days, John. Then you can start your new life." Captain Oliver slapped John on the back.

"In a land where the sun shines only occasionally, and it rains most of the time." George had joined the conversation. "Don't look so worried John, you will get used to it."

Suddenly John rushed towards George, pushed him to the ground and sat on him. "You are a bore George, your jokes about English weather are boring."

EASTMOUNT ESTATE, BARBADOS

FELICITY COULDN'T SLEEP. She tossed and turned, she could still hear the music of the last waltz, still feel Darius's strong arms around her. She felt so guilty. She tried to summon up Arthur's face, but failed. She could only see Darius smiling down at her as he swept her around the ballroom.

When morning came she was up early. As soon as she had bathed and dressed, she slipped out of the house and hurried into the cool of the gardens. The scorching sun that would arrive later was just peeping over the horizon.

As Felicity walked slowly past the rose garden, she thought back on the evening. The opulence of the event had added to her feeling of total detachment from reality. Darius had indeed been charming; his good looks would delight any young woman. In the cool morning, she hoped that her attraction to Darius had been triggered by the music, the wine, and festive atmosphere of the evening. She dreaded seeing Agatha. She knew her sister would be delighted that the meeting between her and Darius had been so successful.

Reluctantly, Felicity returned to the house. Breakfast had been prepared. Agatha was already seated. "My dear you are up already. I was certain that you would still be lying in your bed, dreaming of a certain gentleman." Agatha's bright smile was causing her double chin to wobble.

"I know you mean Darius. He is indeed charming. A wonderful dancing partner."

"More than that I think, Felicity. We are invited to lunch today. I thought the blue. Your hair, I'm not sure. I will come to your room and we can discuss with your maid the best style. Not too formal, but elegant."

Felicity walked to the serving table, took a plate and picked some fruit: cherries, mango and guava. She joined her sister at the breakfast table.

"Agatha, surely the blue is too ornate for a lunch. I think the grey is more appropriate."

"Perhaps you are right. We don't want to look too eager, do we?"

"Eager for what sister?"

"Now don't be silly, we have already discussed just what a wonderful catch Darius would be."

"Agatha, you are forgetting my understanding with Arthur."

"Arthur! And where is he? If he was serious, he would have spoken before he left. Watching you last night I thought you had forgotten all about Arthur."

"Sister, I will accompany you today, out of politeness. Last night was well.... last night." Felicity took a pinch of salt from a small silver pot and sprinkled it on the guava on her plate. "Delicious, I will miss the wonderful fruit we have here when I'm back in England. Have you tried salt on guava?"

"It's not to my taste and don't try to change the subject. Felicity, you must think seriously about your future. Lord Horace was delighted with the way you and Darius seemed to be happy together last night. He told me Darius was enchanted by you."

"Did he?" Despite herself, Felicity felt a flush of pleasure.

BRIDGWATER

MARY'S ENGLISH CONTINUED to improve. It needed to. She was aware that a difficult situation had developed with Tom and Matt Turle. She loved them both, but only as brothers. She missed her brothers and often cried herself to sleep knowing that she would never see them again. Mary now realised that because she missed them, she had spent too much time with the Turle boys. She had been too affectionate. They had misunderstood the signs. She must talk to them. She needed to find the words to make it clear that her fondness for them was not love.

Mary was a sensitive young woman. She felt uncomfortable with the local girls of her own age. When she had first arrived, they had been welcoming. They had made an effort to talk to her using sign language. It had been fun. Now she felt ill at ease with the same young women. She could read their eyes. She was encroaching on their territory. She had deduced that Rachael Maidment adored Tom Turle and it was obvious that Harriet Ridley was in love with Matt. It was time to say what she would have said months ago, if only she had known the words.

Sarah Barham had been vaguely aware that the Turle brothers seemed to spend a lot of time with Mary. Nancy Turle had told her that she was worried that her boys had fallen for Mary, however Sarah was too preoccupied with worry over the missing ship to have given the matter much thought. Now she watched Mary being escorted by Tom and Matt as they headed into town. She smiled to herself. She had heard Mary in her room, practicing what she was going to say to Tom and Matt. Sarah hoped they wouldn't be too upset.

It was market day, and peddlers new to the town and local trades men and women had set up their stalls. Mary enjoyed market day, but in the past she had naively allowed Tom and Matt to buy her little trinkets giving them the wrong impression. She knew she must speak before they reached the market. She stopped; she took them both by the hand. She took a deep breath.

"Tom, Matt there is something I have to say to you both." The young men looked surprised. "I think you are the most wonderful brothers. I miss my brothers." Mary hesitated. The vision of the young men she had been so cruelly taken from loomed before her. She felt tears forming in her eyes. "Thank you for being my brothers." She took another deep breath. "I cannot love you as men. Just as brothers." Mary let go of their hands and stood back, concerned, knowing that she had hurt her good friends.

The two young men appeared offended, then angry. The noise of the market, peddlers calling their wares, excited children's voices, dogs barking, women gossiping were not heard by the three young people standing staring at each other. "Do you understand what I have told you?"

"Only too well." Tom was the first to speak. "Mary, I'm surprised and hurt. I thought we had an understanding."

"So did I. I thought you regarded Tom as a sort of brother, not me. I thought.....Oh God, this is terrible."

"We can still be friends."

"No Mary, we can't." Matt looked close to tears.

"I'm sorry. My English, sometimes I get it wrong. I was too ..." Mary hesitated. "I was too...." She pulled a notebook from her pocket, flipped the pages. "I was too affectionate."

Suddenly, Tom smiled. "Yes, you were Mary, but we have been fools. Come on brother. We have been deluding ourselves. I thought Mary wanted me. You thought she wanted you."

The Reverend Hugh Staunton and his wife Barbara were walking towards them. Mary, Tom and Matt exchanged greetings with them. They waited until they had passed, then Matt turned to his brother.

"I would have fought you for her."

"You would have lost."

"Never, brother. I'll fight you now to prove it."

"I told you, you are just like my brothers. Now stop this nonsense. Tom is right, it is just as well that I have sisterly feelings for you both."

"You are very pretty, Mary. I really did hope that one day...."

"Oh, Matt, thank you. You will still be my brothers?" Mary was smiling. She looked first at Matt, then Tom. She could see they were both trying hard not to show just how upset they were. A minute passed, then Tom spoke.

"Of course. It will be an honour Mary, won't it Matt?"

"Friends." Matt offered Mary his hand. She took it.

"Come, I have my wages, let's spend some money." Mary felt enormous relief. She was delighted that Matt and Tom were still her friends.

LONDON

"DRY LAND! After 60 days. I can't walk properly"

"Neither can I." John caught hold of Thomas's arm for support.

"Let's sit a while. I too find my legs unsteady." Arthur put his travelling bag down.

It had been an emotional farewell to Captain Oliver and his crew. The long voyage and the trauma of the encounter with the Robert Blake had made all on board HMS Lady Cornwall good friends. Addresses had been exchanged, with promises to keep in touch. Arthur and his companions had disembarked before the crew, who had duties to perform before the voyage was over for them.

In amongst the paraphernalia of the docks, Arthur had found a grassy bank to sit on. He stretched his legs out before him. "While you were all celebrating the end of the voyage with the crew, I had a serious conversation with Captain Oliver. He had advised against coach travel. I thought my last experience, traveling from Oxford to Bridgwater was tolerable, but he has discouraged me from trying the London to Exeter run. I know that coach travel is uncomfortable. It's slow and expensive. On top of the fare, passengers are expected to tip the guards and coachmen. You have to pay for food and lodgings. The coachmen on the Exeter run have arrangements with inns along the way, and only stop where they can gain commission. The total cost comes to nearly nine times the basic fare."

"Nine times? Do passengers know that before they board?"

"Captain Oliver says his brother was caught out, that's why he is warning us. I have directions from Captain Oliver to a reputable stable. He has recommended that we travel on horseback with a guide. We will then have freedom of choice when it comes to hostelries."

"I have heard there are highwaymen on the roads in England" Said John with concern.

"There are, but we will be our own men if we come across them, much better to rely on our skills than on the coachmen and guards. We will be armed."

"It sounds exciting. I'm up for a fight with a highway man."

"I think it would be better if we didn't come across them, George. They are evil. Shall we try our legs again?" They staggered to their feet. "The stables Captain Oliver has recommended are a good walk from here. He has advised against the nearest stables. They take advantage of their location close to the docks and price accordingly."

It was obvious that Captain Oliver's recommendation was sound. The condition of the stables and the healthy appearance of the horses was impressive, but it was the owner who immediately put their minds at ease. Benjamin Follett was a West Country man and hearing the familiar soft accent was music to the ears of George, Thomas and Arthur. "My son will be your guide. Jacob, over here. These gentlemen wish to return to the best part of England."

"You mean Somerset father?"

"Of course, my boy." Ben turned to his customers and shrugged his shoulders. "He's a Londoner born and breed, thinks my affection for Somerset is some sort of joke."

"I have the map here father." Jacob had spread the map on a large table. "Just where in the best part of England is your destination, gentlemen?"

"Bridgwater." It was George who spoke.

"Then it will be Windsor, Reading, Newbury, Marlborough, Radstock, Shepton Mallet, Glastonbury and then Bridgwater. We will stop at reputable inns, and, subject to good weather and good luck we should be in Bridgwater in five days' time."

"What about the highway men?"

"John is from Barbados; he has only just learnt about highway men." George explained.

"We will all carry flintlock pistols. We will ride in close formation. It will be up to us all to keep our eyes open for those rascals. I can make no guarantees about the safety of our journey, gentlemen." Jacob looked serious.

"Now, now, Jacob, you know it is unlikely that a group of five men will be attacked." Ben Follett interrupted his son. "A coach would be much more vulnerable. With luck and God's good grace you will have a trouble-free journey. Now, to practicalities. Across the road is a fine inn, not too expensive. I suggest you have a substantial supper followed by a good night's sleep. You will need to be saddled up and ready for departure early in the morning."

Arthur awoke to the sound of rain. He was sharing a room with John, who was also awake. "Your English rain already Arthur."

"Sorry, John. Hopefully it will pass. It's not what we want for the journey."

"I'm cold." John was shivering.

"We will all need to buy warm coats. I have some spare clothes." Arthur rummaged in his bag and pulled out a woolly jumper. He tossed it to John. He pulled out a similar jumper for himself, dressed quickly and turned to see John still in bed.

"Get up, John, I have arranged a breakfast for us all. I'm just going to knock next door to make sure George and Thomas are awake." Before Arthur could reach the door, it opened, and George and Thomas were standing there. George peered into the room and spotted John still in bed. He rushed into the room, caught hold of the side of the mattress and tipped John out of bed. "We have a whole day in the saddle ahead of us, I was just enjoying a few more minutes of comfort." John was indignant.

"John, if George hadn't tipped you out of bed I would have done. We need to eat well before the journey, and we must not be late. The rain is going to slow us. Now get dressed, we will start our breakfasts." Arthur followed George and Thomas down the stairs.

"A good English breakfast, I can smell the bacon. It's great to be home." George was all smiles. The meal was finished off with bread and jam. Jacob joined them just as they had finished eating. They collected their belongings and headed for the stables.

"You will need some warm coats." Jacob eyed his clients with concern. "It's too early for the High Street shop to be open, but I know the owner. Come, lead your horses and follow me." They led the horses out of the stable and trailed behind Jacob. The rain had almost stopped, it was just an unpleasant light drizzle. They walked several hundred yards down a lane and then followed Jacob up the High Street. He stopped in front of Peter Collier and Sons Outfitters and knocked on the door. A few moments later, a window opened, and an angry face appeared. "What the..... oh, it's you Jacob."

"Sorry to wake you, Peter but these gentlemen have just arrived in England from Barbados and are in need of warm coats."

"I was awake, Jacob, I'll come down." The window closed and a few moments later the door to the shop opened. Peter Collier eyed the men standing before him with an expert eye. "Come in, follow me." He moved through the shop to a rack of leather coats and pulled one out of the rack.

"You will need leather to keep out the rain. These are lined with wool. Turn around for me please sir." John turned and felt himself being eased into a coat. He immediately felt the warmth of the wool. He wriggled his shoulders, stretched out his arms and walked to the mirror to admire himself. "It fits, look it's perfect and it's really warm."

"Now one for you." Thomas was the next to be fitted, then Arthur, then George. Peter's expertise in knowing exactly the size of his customers amazed them. "Years of experience." He said with pride.

"Now hats......." A few more minutes were spent on the choice of hats and then Arthur settled the bill and said a quiet thank you to Felicity for her generosity. She had the forethought to provide him money for the English part of the journey. His face was sad as he thought of the beautiful young woman he had left behind. He missed her so much and wondered what she was doing.

EASTMOUNT ESTATE, BARBADOS

IN A GREY SILK dress with her hair arranged in a casual style, suitable for a lunch invitation, Felicity watched Darius with amusement. He was flattering Agatha. Felicity was surprised that her usually intelligent sister was being deceived by the charming young man. Agatha's choice of outfit was far too young for a woman of her age, Felicity knew it and so did Darius.

"Ladies, how wonderful you both look!" Horace Plunkett-Browne had entered the room. Another flatterer thought Felicity. She smiled and offered her hand for Lord Horace to kiss. She saw Darius smiling at her and despite herself, felt her irritation at the falseness of the last few minutes melt away. She took the arm offered by Darius and allowed him to escort her out on to the shaded patio area where a light luncheon had been prepared. The view from the elevated position of the house was superb. In the distance she could see the blue sea was being lightly teased by the wind, causing the waves to be topped with white foam. Close by there was the sound of tiny hummingbirds seeking out nectar in the nearby trees and shrubs. A servant was hovering. When Lord Horace saw her, she spoke to him.

"I'm sorry ladies, it appears that my wife is slightly delayed, a household matter. Oh, here she is." An aristocratic lady entered the room. "I'm so sorry I'm late." Lady Iris looked flustered. "That breeze is most welcome."

The servant helped the ladies to be seated and poured the wine.

"I will miss this beautiful island." Darius was appreciating the view.

"Are you to return soon to England?" Agatha looked surprised. Felicity noticed that Lord Horace looked perturbed.

"Darius is here for as long as he likes. We love having you here my boy."

"It can be a little quiet for a young man used to the society of London, Horace." Felicity was curious, Lady Iris seemed to irritate her husband with her remark.

"Don't forget in London I wouldn't have the charming company of Miss Felicity."

"Well said my boy. Well said indeed." Felicity struggled not to laugh at Lord Horace's fatuous smile, instead she smiled modestly. She was amused by how silly and contrived the exchange had been.

More small talk followed but Felicity's mind was elsewhere. She was fighting with her emotions. She was still disappointed that Arthur had decided to travel to England. She had struggled to understand and felt hurt that he was prepared to leave her for so long. Darius was in so many ways the perfect husband for her. Rich, a member of the aristocracy, handsome, charming in a way befitting his class. Marriage to Darius would please her family.

She had been surprised that Lord Plunkett-Browne and Agatha had so readily agreed to Arthur's return to England. She could see clearly now that her sister was determined that she would never be Arthur's wife.

"Felicity, you appear to be miles away." Darius was looking at her intently.

"I'm sorry, it was rude of me. I was just thinking how much I too would miss this beautiful island, I have only a matter of weeks before my visit here will be over." She saw the delighted expression on her sister's face. She had decided to play Agatha at her own game.

"Miss Felicity must not be allowed to travel unaccompanied. Darius, you must return with Miss Felicity to ensure her safety. One never knows what misfortune may befall a gentile young lady on the high seas."

"What a sensible idea Lord Horace." Agatha was beaming her approval.

"Then it is decided. Felicity and Darius will return to England together." Lord Horace was delighted. Felicity felt Darius's gaze on her and found herself blushing.

A FEW MILES FROM GLASTONBURY

"MY REAR END is sore. How much longer?"

"We should be at the inn in about a quarter of an hour. Try standing in the saddle." Jacob responded.

"I have done, but then my legs get tired and I have to sit down, and then my rear end feels even more sore."

"George, we are all uncomfortable. I'm surprised you are complaining so much. Compared to weeks below deck in a stinking ship, tossing and turning with men crying and vomiting all around us, this is paradise."

"But that was then, Thomas, this is now."

"Just think of that tankard of ale waiting for us and a hearty meal followed by a firm bed with a soft pillow."

They travelled on for a few moments in silence, all thinking about the pleasant evening before them. They were nearing the end of their journey. They had been lucky with the weather and Jacob's choice of inns had pleased them all.

The road was through a thick forest, the light of day almost obliterated by the dense foliage above them. They rounded a corner and hurriedly pulled on their reins, forcing their mounts to a halt. In front of them was a carriage, the passengers were in the process of dismounting at gunpoint. It was a hold-up! Two highwaymen; still mounted were waving their guns at the terrified travellers. There was a moment's silence as all concerned took in the new development. One of the highwaymen moved towards the new arrivals. "Stay exactly where you are and throw down your guns."

"It's a woman!" George exclaimed. In his excitement he

spurred his horse forward.

"George, stop!" Thomas called out. There was the sound of a flintlock pistol firing. The coach passengers were facing George and they saw a surprised expression on his face, then he slumped forward, and his startled horse reared. John had the presence of mind to lean across and grab the reins while at the same time holding his own horse steady. He had seen where the bullet had hit George, he knew he was dead.

"I say again your guns! Now." The high-pitched female voice was wavering. She was pointing her other gun; and had it cocked ready to shoot. Thomas, who was driven by anger to act without thought of danger, raised his gun and shot the woman in the arm. Her companion, confused, momentarily lowered her gun, and Jacob urged his mount forward and charged straight at her. Her mount reared up in fear and dislodged its rider. By now Arthur had dismounted and was standing over the injured woman, his gun pointed at her as she writhed in agony on the ground. The stagecoach guard had retrieved his own gun and stood over the other felon.

"John, take over. I need to attend to George." Arthur rushed to where George had fallen and saw the gaping head wound.

"How is he?" It was Thomas who asked. Arthur turned and took in the scene before him, he saw that the coachman and male passengers were now fully involved in tying up the two women. He walked slowly over to Thomas. Thomas saw the expression on Arthur's face. He pushed passed Arthur and fell weeping by the body of his friend.

The male passengers rushed to help the coachmen. The women, most of them weeping, comforted each other. They stood shocked by the scene before them. A matter of minutes before they had been frightened for their own safety, now they were witnesses to the heart-breaking distress of the dead man's companions.

It was only a few miles to the inn that had been recommended by Jacob. He led the way, settled his clients in and returned to the scene of the murder, taking responsibility for the body and to assist the coachmen.

THE NEXT MORNING

"IT IS FORTUNATE that George's family live this side of Bridgwater. We can avoid riding through the town with his body."

"The women?"

"The coach guard will take them to the watchman. There was a coachful of witnesses, the women will hang." Arthur's voice was harsh, he heard the whinnying of a horse behind him, he turned, and saw Thomas. He looked a defeated man. He could not believe that his funny, cheerful friend who had survived the battle of Sedgemoor, transportation and slavery would be killed by a woman in a forest 20 miles from home.

"Keep close to me, I don't want Thomas to hear what we are saying." Jacob steered his mount nearer to Arthur's horse. "I don't think it would be wise for Thomas to see the family first. They will be overjoyed, and think George is with him. It can't be Thomas who tells them, he would break down, he is close to tears now. You and John must keep him back, you must be forceful. Ride far enough behind me to avoid being seen when we get close to the farm."

"Do the family know you?"

"They are part of my father's congregation. They know me as the vicar's son."

"They will be puzzled as to why you are calling on them, do they know you went to Barbados?"

"I presume so, when they see me, they might well think there is something wrong. They may have a minute to prepare themselves for bad news. It will have to be me." Arthur sounded resolute, but he was panicking. He dreaded telling the Carrow family their George was dead.

The Carrow farm was small but successful. Mr Carrow had been able to afford a sound education for his three sons, and had obtained an apprenticeship for George, his eldest, with a master carpenter. Mrs Carrow had quite naturally been dismayed when George had told them that he was to march with Monmouth, but her husband had told her that, if he was younger and without the responsibility for his family, he would have marched. The news of their son's captivity and transportation had been greeted with an element of relief. So many families had lost their boys, at least George was still alive. The news that the new monarchs had pardoned the survivors of the rebellion had brought joy to their hearts. They waited every day for news of their son's return.

Mr Carrow was in the yard when Arthur rode up. His arrival had set off the farm dogs who were suspicious of all strangers.

It was the worst day of Arthur's life. He would always remember the look of surprised on Mr Carrow's weather beaten face, then the flicker of alarm as he wondered why the vicar's son who should have been in Barbados had ridden into his yard. Arthur had dismounted; he walked up to Mr Carrow and offered his hand.

"It's George isn't it? Somethings happened to George." Mr Carrow saw the sad expression of Arthur's face.

"I'm so sorry, Mr Carrow, George is dead." Mr Carrow swayed, looking for a few moments as if he would fall. He had a moment of acceptance. His best mate Jeremiah Slade had lost both his sons at Sedgemoor, why should he escape the anguish of losing a child? Then he felt despair, to lose George now when they expected him home, safe and sound, was harsh, it would devastate his family. He knew he must steady himself, he stared at Arthur for a few moments. He needed to be strong.

"I'll tell my wife." Mr Carrow turned on his heels and walked towards the farmhouse.

It had been agreed that after 10 minutes Thomas would enter the farmhouse. He knew the family well and they were well aware that it had been George's idea for them to join the rebellion. Thomas had that consolation. It would have been impossible for him to try to comfort the family if he had encouraged George to fight. They watched Thomas spur his horse forward with heavy hearts.

After ten more minutes Arthur led the horse carrying George's dead body into the yard. He tethered the horse and then entered the house. The sound of sobbing led him to the room where the family were assembled. Mr Carrow, who had been sitting comforting his wife, rose when he saw Arthur. He swiftly crossed the room. "Thomas has told us the details; you have bought my boy home?"

Arthur struggled to find his voice, he failed. He just nodded and led the father to his child.

Feeling wretched, the travellers left Thomas with the Carrow family, they rode on in silence, each with their own thoughts. The shocking events of the day would live with them forever.

As they approached Bridgwater, despite themselves, their spirits lifted. For John it was the realisation that this was the town where he could possibly spend the rest of his life. For Jacob, it was relief that his job as guide was over. For Arthur it meant that he would see his family again. John and Jacob stopped off at the Three Mariners, where they would spend the night, thankful to get out of the saddle.

Arthur now faced another daunting task. He had to tell his father that a man he admired and respected was a murderer. As he entered the town, he saw some surprised faces as he was recognised. He briefly acknowledged greetings and hastened to the vicarage. He dismounted in the yard, and before he could ring the bell the door was thrown open by his sister Anne, she threw her arms around him. "You came, it's a miracle! Mother, father, Arthur's here." Arthur gently released himself from this sister's embrace and saw the astonished faces of his parents.

"Arthur, I can't believe it, we didn't think the letter would get to you in time." His mother smothered him with kisses. When she released him, it was his father's turn to embrace him.

"To my study my boy, we have much to talk about." He had Arthur by the elbow and steered him away from the excited chatter of his wife and daughter. Once in the study, Hugh Staunton closed the door. "Now my boy, your mother and sister are too excited to think clearly, but I know it's not possible for you to have received the letter telling you of Jane's wedding in time for you to return for the event."

Arthur was stunned, Jane's wedding! He hadn't lied to Lord Horace and Lady Agatha. His sister was getting married.

"Are you in trouble? Have you lost your job?"

"No father, I am to return as soon as possible." Arthur hesitated. He was just about to continue when there was frantic knocking on the door. Hugh looked irritated, but he stood up and opened the door. It was his wife Barbara.

"Sorry, Hugh but you must come. It's the caterers, they say they can't supply enough wine." Hugh made an inaudible comment and hurried to the hall. Barbara smiled at her son.

"I can't believe you are here, it's the most wonderful thing." They could hear raised voices in the hall, Jane had heard of the supply problem and was making her concern known. Then the study door opened, and Jane flew in.

"I've just heard! Arthur thank you for coming all the way from Barbados for my wedding. Oh, my wonderful brother!" Once again Arthur was smothered with kisses.

"Jane, I need you, we must make a decision about the wine." It was Hugh calling. Jane hurried out of the room.

"Arthur my dear, it is a miracle that you are here." Barbara now looked serious. "You must have been shocked by the news about Sir Samuel." Arthur looked confused. It took a couple of seconds to understand that the letter telling of Jane's wedding must have contained other news. It was fortunate that Barbara was studying her hands and didn't notice her son's confusion.

"I know you will want to talk to your father about his passing. You were very close to him." The door opened, and Hugh entered the room.

"Problem solved, but the solution is expensive." Hugh smiled. "Just as well I only have two daughters. Barbara, I need to talk to Arthur."

"I understand." Barbara left them.

"Now my boy, what has happened to cause you to leave your position and travel for weeks to return home. It must be something serious."

"It was, but now it seems that fate has played a hand. Father, I lied to Lady Eastmount, I told her I had to return for my sister's wedding."

"But you couldn't have known."

"I didn't. But I needed a reason to return. Father, mother has told me that Sir Samuel has passed away."

"That is correct."

"The reason I returned was because I know he killed Molly Fisher."

"And you said nothing!" Hugh was astonished.

"Father, I have agonised over this. It was the day Eliza rejected me. I had been drinking, I had taken a fall and knocked my head. My mind was in turmoil. I blocked the memory. It was a scarf that made me remember. I saw Sir Samuel dabbing his face with a woman's scarf. It was the same scarf Molly had been wearing. There was blood on Sir Samuel's face. Sir Samuel saw me, I had waved at him, but he turned away from me. I remember the expression on his face. He was horrified that I had seen him. Father, I know how this sounds…."

"My boy, calm yourself. Your suspicion was correct. Sir Samuel did kill Mollie Fisher, Mable Finnimore, James Plomer and Jenny Norris. He confessed and stated in his letter that he intended to kill himself." Hugh regarded his son with concern, he looked ill. Just then there was a knock on the door. Hugh let out a sigh and opened the door. It was Barbara.

"I'm so sorry Hugh, the caterers had forgotten to ask about the soup, what did you decide, I preferred…." The door closed, and Arthur was left to his thoughts. He felt tremendous relief. He had made a pointless journey but had avoided the chaos his memory would have brought to his father and the community if Sir Samuel hadn't confessed. Then he remembered, the Robert Blake. He still had responsibilities to fulfil before he could enjoy his sister's wedding. He thought of Felicity, he wished she was with him, he felt an ache in his heart that he knew wouldn't go away until they were together again.

He then felt guilty. He had failed to tell his father the terrible news about George. His father had returned. "Sorry Arthur, this wedding…. my boy what's wrong?" Arthur tried to tell Hugh but found that his voice had failed him. When he could speak and blurted out the details of George's murder he found himself sobbing in his father's arms as the events of the past two days overwhelmed him.

***

ARTHUR'S MOTHER AND sisters were rushing around the house on various errands to do with the impeding nuptials. His father had excused himself and hurried to the church to attend to some urgent business. Arthur went to his old room and took a few moments to sit on the bed and inspect the childhood items still in the room or on the wall. He found a change of clothes and then washed off the dust of the journey.

Feeling refreshed and composed, he found the maid and told

her to tell his mother that he had business to attend to, but he would be back to join the family for supper. As he approached the stables it occurred to him that his horse Arrow might not recognise him. He was wrong and was greeted with loud whinnying and stamping of hoofs. It took both the stable boy and Arthur to calm the excited horse.

Back in the saddle again Arthur finally managed to ease himself into a comfortable position. Fortunately, he knew he didn't have far to travel. He had decided his first stop should be to deliver Captain Kemplyn's letter to his wife. He stayed longer than intended. Betty Kemplyn sobbed with relief when she read the letter and fired questions at Arthur he couldn't answer. He felt helpless; all he could add to the information in the letter was that her husband was well when he last saw him. As to when he would return, the obvious question for his wife to ask, he had no idea. He finally managed to leave by explaining to her that he had to hasten to Barham Manor to inform William Barham of the whereabouts of his ship. He assured her that once William Barham had the information that the ship had headed to the African coast, he should be able to track her. He wasn't at all sure that was true, but what he said reassured Betty and he was able to leave.

***

"THE ROBERT BLAKE IN Africa!" William Barham was incredulous. "You say she was hijacked by slaves. I can't believe it. Was she sound when you saw her?"

"She was sound and Captain Kemplyn appeared to have a good relationship with the slaves. He gave me a letter for the Pemberton-Harvey trading company. Jacob, who was our guide will deliver it them in Bristol."

"So, the Pemberton-Harveys will know the result of their dishonesty. Thank you, Arthur, for bringing me this news. I must ride to inform my cousin Edward who is my business partner and then tell the families of the crew that there is still hope that their loved ones will survive." Suddenly William looked at Arthur with a quizzical expression on his face. "My boy, how rude of me. I was so overwhelmed with your news of the Robert Blake that it didn't occur to me to ask you why you have returned."

"It was for my sister's wedding." Arthur smiled as he said it.

"But that's not possible. Your father told me that it was regretful that by the time the letter telling you of the event arrived in Barbados the wedding would have already taken place. Your family didn't expect you to return."

"William, my father has told me about the passing of Sir Samuel. It's a long story, and I know you have errands to run, but the fact is I remembered seeing something. I knew Sir Samuel was a murderer. That's why I returned."

"You knew?" William looked shocked.

"I knew, I will explain when you have more time." He could see that William was anxious to leave.

"I would wish to hear your story now, but I must go. Tomorrow?"

"I will call at 10.00."

"Ten o'clock it is then." Both men hurried out of the house and mounted their horses. As they parted Arthur could sense a chill in William's attitude towards him. Arthur was pleased that they would be meeting again the follow morning and then he could explain himself fully.

BARBADOS

LORD PLUNKET- BROWNE refilled his glass. He really shouldn't be drinking red wine in this heat he thought, especially in the afternoon. He would make it the last one, at least until dinner time. He sat back in his comfortable chair and enjoyed the wine.

He had finished writing two letters. One was to Agatha Eastmount inviting her and Felicity to a cricket match the following day, the other to his sister-in-law in England. He smiled to himself. That young doctor was so grateful when I agreed to him returning to England for his sister's wedding, he thought. He picked up the decanter, just half a glass this time, then no more. He took sip of the wine, then he rolled the parchment, melted the sealing wax, sealed the documents, wrapped red ribbon around them and marked one to be added to other correspondence to his sister-in-law, and one to Lady Eastmount.

***

AGATHA COULD HEAR the shrill voice of Sophie Bagwell-Giles. "My point!" Felicity was playing tennis with Sophie and her brother Percy. Felicity was partnered by Darius. Agatha took a few moments to watch the match. Darius was looking devastatingly handsome as he moved elegantly around the court. It was obvious that Sophie had taken a shine to him. Darius was playing a smart game of tennis, but also another clever game. He was with great delicacy using Sophie's admiration for him to make Felicity jealous. As Agatha watched, he knelt before Sophie and kissed her hand. It was an exaggerated gesture to congratulate her on her last shot. The match would soon be finishing, Agatha thought. It had started in the cool of the morning but now the sun must be making the game unpleasant.

Agatha moved to her office in the coolest part of the house. There were times she wished herself back in England. The heat was overwhelming, she loosened her corset, and sat at her desk to deal with some letters that had been delivered. She sorted the correspondence and brushed aside the obvious requests for payment. Her eyes rested on the scroll with the seal of Lord Plunkett-Browne. She unrolled the parchment and started to read. The self-satisfied expression on her face quickly darkened to anger. She finished reading the letter, and then re-read it. Her first glance had caught sight of her name in the body of the letter and her curiosity to read more had led her to missing the fact that the letter was addressed to someone named Charlotte.

Agatha felt faint, she rang the bell, and when the servant arrived, she requested a large glass of chilled wine. She could hear the voices of the tennis players calling out for cool drinks. She thought about how she had encouraged Felicity. She had trusted her own class, the educated and monied class. She saw things on the island that disturbed her, in her heart she knew that her husband's wealth and status came from the humiliation and toil of others, but she toed the line. She lived and thought as she had been taught. In her ignorance she would never have believed that Lord Horace would deceive her. I have been taken for a fool, she thought. She felt tears filling her eyes. The affront to her family was extraordinary. Lord Plunkett-Browne had been cold and calculating in his strategy. It was Felicity's money he and his nephew Darius were after. The letter was making it clear to Charlotte, who Agatha realised was Lord Horace's sister-in-law, mother of Darius, that Lord Horace had borrowed heavily to give the impression of enormous wealth to impress her and Felicity.

He boasted in the letter that Darius had been successful in charming the young heiress Felicity. He wrote that her troublesome penny less Darius would very soon be married to real money. All his gambling debts would be paid, and the unpleasant problem of the child would be resolved. Agatha put the letter down. She was muttering to herself. "I've been taken for a fool and I've allowed my little sister to be taken for a fool." She felt the sting of more tears in her eyes when she read again Lord Horace's description of her. Agatha wept. A few moments later Agatha smiled. So, Lord Plunkett-Browne was short of money was he? Her husband would no doubt be delighted with that piece of information.

***

"OH AGATHA, WE had the most exciting game. Darius and I thought we had Sophie and her brother beaten three times, but they kept fighting back. But we won in the end!" Felicity looked hot but happy.

"I'm pleased for you Felicity. I'm also please that you have finished your match. It's far too hot to be playing tennis."

"I know, but we just had to finish the game. Darius is a wonderful player..... what's wrong Agatha. I can tell by your face that something bad has happened."

Agatha handed the letter to Felicity. "Read it, as soon as you have finished, I must get it taken to the quay. There is a sailing for England departing this evening."

Felicity read the letter. Several times she looked at her sister, her eyes wide with astonishment. "Oh Agatha, I'm so sorry. We have been taken for fools."

"You are not upset? I expected tears." Agatha was surprised by Felicity's reaction.

"I am relieved. I will be honest with you; I was falling for Darius. It made me feel guilty, but I was angry with Arthur for leaving me. I know it sounds stupid, but I had a dream. Arthur had told me that he had been hoping to marry but the girl found another love whilst he was studying at Oxford. I dreamt that he met the girl when he was back in England, and she was still single. They fell in love again."

"My dear girl." The usually cold Agatha hugged her sister warmly. Felicity sniffed, then found a handkerchief and blew her nose.

"Arthur left me a letter. He made me promise that I would wait two months until I read it. He joked that he wanted me to wait because he thought that by that time I might have forgotten him. I broke my promise and read it this morning. I needed assurance after the dream. When I read what Arthur had written I fell in love with him all over again." Felicity waved Lord Plunkett-Browne's letter, she looked angry. "Until I read this appalling letter, I still had a fondness for Darius. Agatha, I am aware that you promised mother that you would ensure that I made a good match, but I feel I have had a lucky escape."

"I am relieved. I was worried you would feel hurt. We will talk later when you have bathed as you must be hot from tennis. I must hasten to make sure my husband gets this letter."

"Robert?" Felicity looked puzzled.

"Yes, it is clear from the letter that the Plunkett-Browne's have money problems. Robert will know what to do to avenge the insult to our family."

Felicity left the room and Agatha quickly wrote a note to her husband. She bound both Lord Horace's letter and her note together and sealed them with wax. She rang a bell for a servant and instructed him to get the letter to the dock for transportation to England.

She knew Lord Horace's letter intended for her would be sent to his sister-in-law and she would most certainly return it to Lord Horace asking for an explanation. Lord Horace would eventually realise his error. She had months to have some fun with Lord Horace and get revenge. Then she had a sudden thought. "Oh no!" she said to herself. "I wonder what was in the letter intended for me?" Agatha sat for a few moments and then picked up her pen. She wrote a note of apology to Lord Horace. She explained that a letter had arrived from him but unfortunately her naughty puppy Tinker had picked it up when it had fallen off a table and had run away with it. It hadn't been found.

BRIDGWATER

THERE WAS SO much going that on that week that Hugh Staunton had struggled to comprehend what Arthur was telling him. "He is my friend, father, he was a great help to me when I first arrived in Barbados."

"You say he was a slave."

"He was born to a slave. He is now a free man."

"And he wants to teach. Does he have any experience?"

"None at all, but he was tutored by his father, an educated Irish rebel. He is a better mathematician than I am. He is personable, friendly and willing to learn. Please

father, persuade the headmaster to give him a chance." The hall clock struck, indicating the half hour. "I must leave, I have to be at Barham House by 10.00. Can you speak to the headmaster?"

"I will go immediately. Roger will be surprised, but he is a sensible man. I am sure he will give John a chance....." Hugh stopped speaking as he was interrupted by a fracas of some sort going on in the hall. They could hear Barbara demanding that her daughters sort out their disagreement without disturbing the entire household. Hugh looked resigned. "Only one more day to go my boy, then the chaos caused by the wedding preparations will be over." He smiled when he said it. "When will your friend arrive?"

"He is staying at the Three Mariners. I have told him to come here at 2.00. When I have finished my business with William I will come back here. Hopefully, by then you will have news for me regarding the teaching position. I must away father, I can't be late." Arthur hurried to the stables.

As he had expected, Arthur received a rather frosty welcome from William Barham. He understood William's astonishment that Arthur had suspected Sir Samuel of being a murderer. After half an hour Arthur took his leave. William was now totally sympathetic. He commended Arthur for his decision to return to England to ensure that a man he admired faced justice. In a happier frame of mind, Arthur spurred his horse and rode back to town.

He was sitting with his father in the study when there was a knock at the door. The door was opened by the maid Angela who was blushing as she smiled at the visitor. Hugh and Arthur stood up. "Father, let me introduce you to John Fitzpatrick, John, this is my father Hugh Staunton."

Hugh extended his hand in welcome, then a smile spread across his face when the young man acknowledged his greeting in a soft Irish accent. Hugh gestured to the armchairs. "Please sit, Arthur has told me that you are game enough to take on the rather onerous task of teaching at the grammar school."

"Don't say onerous, father. I have been telling him that it will be the most gratifying experience."

"I was joking John and I must admit it was a foolish joke. Arthur must have told you that we lost three teachers at the Battle of Sedgemoor. I, myself, have been assisting the remaining staff. I have spoken to the headmaster Roger French this morning. He is anxious to meet you. Come; let us leave this mad house. I can hear my daughters arguing again." He led the way. It was only a short distance to the school.

King James Grammar School had been where the illustrious Robert Blake had been educated. The arrival of Hugh and Arthur accompanied by John Fitzpatrick was noticed by the students who were all curious. Who was the tall, dark skinned man? Roger French had already informed his staff that John would be joining them. There was relief. The dedicated teachers were delighted that there would be another teacher. However, their enthusiasm had dimmed when they discovered that the newcomer had no teaching experience. Hugh and Arthur left John at the school. Roger wanted John to meet the rest of the staff at the end of the school day.

To John's relief he found the teachers welcoming and it was suggested that a good way to get to know each other was over a glass of ale. The young men settled themselves in the bar of the Three Mariners where John was staying. They were fascinated by John's stories of life in Barbados and the sea journey back to England. The pleasant, friendly atmosphere of the evening dissipated when the subject of George's sad death was mentioned. The discussion then changed to the more serious matters of the school curriculum and giving John an insight into the ability and behaviour of the pupils. It had been decided that John would spend at least a week observing. He was to make a start the following day. When his new colleagues bade him farewell he had learnt much about the school and the boys.

**

IN THE MORNING John had spent some time standing before the mirror in his bedroom practicing a stern look. He could remember the look his father used to give him when he had misbehaved. Before he left for school he bade farewell to Jacob who was returning to London.

John was to take up residence in a small cottage in the school grounds. He had packed his belongings, settled his bill and set off for the school. He was welcomed by the headmaster who introduced him to the boys at assembly. John had quelled the tittering in the hall his appearance had caused with the stern look. He was pleased with the immediate effect it had on the boys.

After assembly he had observed English, history and geography lessons. He was impressed with the overall intelligence of the boys and the skill of the teachers. He had stayed behind at the end of classes at the request of the headmaster. He had a short conversation with him and assured him that he had enjoyed the whole experience and was looking forward to tomorrow.

He decided to explore the town, and quickly found himself walking along the riverbank. The tide was out, and the river Parrett was looking its worst. Even at high tide with the sun shining on the water it would look miserable to a native of Barbados. John sighed, he remembered the teasing he had received from Thomas and George. George, he felt a tug at his heart. He hadn't seen Thomas since they had left him with the Carrow family.

He was suddenly aware of a female figure walking towards him. He felt surprised, what was an African woman doing walking along a riverbank in Bridgwater?

***

JANE STAUNTON'S VISIT to Norfolk to find a husband had proved successful. Hugh's cousin Jeremiah had introduced Jane to many eligible young men who had all found Jane enchanting. Jane was fully aware that the visit to her uncle was initiated by her father who was concerned that she could end up an old maid. She had felt irritated and had intended to be uncooperative but in fact she had enjoyed herself. One young man in particular had attracted her attention. His name was Daniel Nash.

The Nash family had now arrived in Bridgwater. They were staying at the Rose and Crown. Barbara Staunton had hurried to the inn as soon as she received news of their arrival. She fussed around, anxious that they had everything they needed until David Nash, Daniel's father insisted she sat down, relax and enjoy a glass of wine with him and his wife. The Nash family were well to do, good Protestants and delighted that they were going to welcome Jane into their family.

***

HUGH STRUGGLED WITH his emotions as he officiated at the marriage of his eldest daughter. As the young couple exchanged their vows, he smiled at his beloved Barbara who was dabbing the tears away from her eyes.

There was a reception for all the guests and dancing in the Town Hall for the town folk. Many of the younger guests made their way to the Town Hall, attracted by the music.

Arthur, still shaken by the murder of George had persuaded Thomas and John to join him at the Town Hall. He told them he had no stomach for celebration but, as the brother of the bride he had to be cheerful on her special day. He asked them if they would help him. He needed his friends' support. He was the vicar's son and it was expected that he would dance with the local ladies. He told them that George, a man who would never turn down the opportunity of having a good time would approve.

Thomas stood and watched the jolly throng. He had been amused by Arthur's devotion to duty. Already he had danced with three different girls. John, who was as reluctant as Thomas had been to attend the dance was partnering Arthur's sister Anne and was obviously enjoying her company. Thomas was suddenly aware that a young woman was close to him.

"In my country it is acceptable for a woman to ask a man to dance." Thomas was astonished. She was beautiful. Tall and slim, her dark skin complementing the rich blue gown she was wearing. She had a strong lilting accent. One he recognised from his island prison.

"I'm Mary, I work for Mr and Mrs Barham. You must excuse my English, I'm still learning."

"Your English is excellent. I'm Thomas."

"I must confess, I do know who you are, and I know you are sad. Come…" Mary held his hand and gently pulled him towards the dancing. "There is nothing like dancing to cheer the spirit."

***

A HAPPY EVENT, the wedding of the vicar's daughter, was followed two days later by the funeral of George Carrow.

Since the delivery of their son's body to their home the windows and mirrors, even bowls of water in the farmhouse had been covered in black cloth. Jewellery was hidden and dull fabric was used for mourning clothes. There was a superstition that any shiny object might attract the spirit of the departed and keep him earthbound.

George's body had been wrapped in a winding sheet made of wool. King Charles II had introduced a law that the departed must be buried dressed in wool in an attempt to support the English wool trade.

The coffin was made of oak, painted black. To avoid the unpleasant smell of bodily fluids, the interior had been covered with a thick layer of bran to soak up any moisture.

Funeral cards illustrated with pictures of gravestones and skeletons had been sent out to friends and the extended family. John was shocked when he received his. Thomas explained to him that the custom was not intended to be morbid, but it was to remind the living that all must at some time pass away.

On the day of the funeral a cart bearing the coffin set off on its journey to the church. The funeral party walked behind the cart, all wearing black.

Throughout the service the sound of sobbing could be heard. George, funny cheerful George had been popular. Many cried because of the loss of the young man but also there was sadness that he had died just when he thought his ordeal was over.

The Carrow family had selected a pleasant spot in the graveyard. The Reverend Hugh Staunton's voice was shaking when he said the final prayer and George's coffin was lowered into the ground. Hugh looked up from his prayer book and saw Mr Carrow and his wife, their faces haggard with grief. They moved forward and Mr Carrow picked up a handful of earth and gave some to his wife. They tossed it on to coffin, then walked away, Mr Carrow supporting his heart broken wife.

All who attended the funeral were invited back to the Carrow farmhouse for wine and biscuits.

BARHAM MANOR

"FATHER, I'VE WORKED it out!" Paul entered his father's study without knocking.

"What's the hurry young man?"

"Look father, look at my calculations." Paul wanted to spread out a piece of parchment on his father's desk.

"Just a moment, I will make room." William removed his work to make space for Paul.

"John told me that they came across the Robert Blake during a storm. They had left Barbados on 17 April and they met up with Robert Blake on 9th May. Robert Blake then had to sail to Africa. We don't know exactly the destination in Africa, but we can estimate that it would be between 1800 to 2000 nautical miles. That would be three to four weeks at sea. The return journey would be 2500 – 2700 nautical miles. That could be four to six weeks at sea, depending on the wind. We don't know how long the ship will need to stay in Africa, but it's possible that the Robert Blake could be back by September."

"My boy, I'm impressed. Did you work this out all by yourself?"

"No father, I must confess that John helped me. I have learnt that a mile is .86 of a nautical mile."

"This is good work Paul. Can I keep these calculations?"

"Of course, father." Paul was looking extremely pleased with himself.

"I will show them to Edward tomorrow. It will help us with planning the business." William looked cheerful. "I do hope you are right. Back by September! It would be wonderful."

THE EASTMOUNT ESTATE BARBADOS.

IT TURNED OUT that the missing letter had been an invitation to a cricket match. A sporting event arranged to show off Darius's ability as a sportsman. He was an excellent cricketer, accomplished as both a bowler and batsman. Felicity was suitably impressed as was Sophie Bagwell-Giles.

Agatha and Felicity had hatched a plan. Felicity was to continue flirting with Darius. She was to keep him at arm's length but make him believe that it was still her intention to travel back to England with him. Lord Plunkett-Browne presumed that they would travel back as an engaged couple. Felicity had great fun in making sure that she was never alone with Darius thus never giving him the opportunity to speak.

In the past, the sisters had not been close. Now, as conspirators they found they liked each other; they had the same sense of mischief. Felicity was astonished at just how devious her sister could be.

THE VICARAGE BRIDGWATER

HAVING ATTENDED HIS sister's wedding and George's funeral Arthur was ready to return to Barbados. He felt sad for his mother. Barbara had been understandably distressed when Jane and her new husband left for their new home in Norfolk. She had pleaded with him to stay longer, but he had been firm. He felt uncomfortable because he knew that if his plans went as he hoped they would, his mother would miss his wedding.

He still had two years of his contract to fulfil and he could not wait that long to marry Felicity. He knew that his mother Barbara would wish for at least one of her children to settle in Bridgwater and it looked as if her wish would be granted. It was obvious that John was in love with his sister Anne, and Anne felt the same for John. Arthur would be delighted to have John as a brother-in-law.

With the Barham shipping company's schedule being in disarray because of the missing Robert Blake, Arthur had to travel to Bristol to find a ship bound for Barbados. After the horrific murder of George, Barbara and Hugh had insisted that Arthur travel to Bristol by coach. There was now an extra guard allotted for all journeys.

There was a small gathering to see Arthur depart. His parents and sister Anne, Mr and Mrs Barham and their two boys. John and Thomas and Thomas's friend Mary. Just as Arthur was about to board the coach, he saw Mr and Mrs Carrow and their sons hurrying towards him. They wished him well.

ON BOARD THE ROBERT BLAKE

CAPTAIN KEMPLYN WAS beginning to think that his long voyage might soon be over. The freed slaves had kept their word and had allowed him and his crew to sail home. The twins Abraham and Matthew had decided to stay in Africa. They had both formed relationships with pretty young women and had ambitious plans for life back home. Many a night he sat with his crew and they speculated about the future of the freed slaves they had left behind. All worried for them but agreed that they had their freedom and it had been their decision to settle in what could still be a dangerous country for them.

There was a knock on his cabin door, and his first lieutenant entered. He advised him that they were approaching the Azores.

The harbour of Ponta Delgada was busy. The Robert Blake had to ride at anchor for several hours before they could come alongside the quay. It was comforting to be amongst people again. The noise and colours of the quayside were exhilarating.

"Ahoy there!"   The voice was coming from a ship anchored close to them. Captain Kemplyn acknowledged the call. He walked to the bow of his ship. The captain of the other ship who had called him was standing at the stern of his vessel.

"Captain Jones at your service sir."

"Captain Kemplyn, how can I help you Captain Jones?"

"As you are the Robert Blake out of Bridgwater, I presume that is where you are heading."

"That is correct."

"We have Somerset men on board. Prisoners released on the order of the King and Queen. I am bound for London. It would make sense if you took the Somerset men on board.

"I would be honoured to do so sir." Some of the crew of the Robert Blake had heard the exchange and excited chatter broke out. They all knew men who had been transported. "When can they come aboard?"

"As soon as it is convenient for you."

"Bring them now. We have to buy some basic provisions – more than we expected it would seem." Captain Kemplyn was laughing. "Captain Jones, how many men?"

"I'm not sure."

"Don't worry, we will count them as they come aboard."

BARHAM MANOR

"IT'S INTERESTING SARAH but it seems that the turbulence of the last decade has taught the people of Bridgwater to take life as it comes. A brown skinned man from Barbados with an Irish accent with no teaching experience is proving to be a gift from God." William and Sarah were sitting in the library, Sarah was slightly irritated that William had finished reading his newssheet and had interrupted her enjoyment of the book she was reading.

"I was speaking to Roger French yesterday, and he is delighted with John's performance. After one week of observation, John took the plunge and started teaching. The students love him. Roger is an experienced headmaster, but he has been impressed with John's quick mind. He told me John's life experience fascinates the boys. It seems Paul is not the only boy eager to go to school now."

They heard the sound of horses' hooves outside the window. Then there was a knock on the door followed by an exchange of words; William was up on his feet and hurried to find out the nature of the visit. Sarah, realising the time, moved to the kitchen to discuss the day's dinner menu with the cook. Cook was just wiping her hands on a towel, ready to sit with her mistress when the kitchen door burst open.

"Great news!" William rushed into the kitchen. "I've just received word that the Robert Blake has been spotted close to the Scilly Isles that means God willing they could be home within a week."

"Oh William, that's wonderful."

"Pemberton-Harvey was advised by the captain of a ship that docked in Bristol. All ships have been on alert for a sighting for months. Clive's brother sent a messenger to notify me."

"The least he could do."

"You have never said a truer word. I must contact Captain Kemplyn's wife and the families of the other seamen. We will just have to pray that the ship finishes the final leg of the journey safely."

EASTMOUNT ESTATE, BARBADOS

"I HAVE JUST come from Lord Horace. The plan is that you sail on Tuesday on the merchant ship Flying Fox. The silly man has even paid for your ticket!"

"Oh Agatha, we have taken the deception too far. I must make my situation clear to Darius now."

"No! Remember that insulting letter. On the journey back I formed a plan. You will pack your travel bags and travel with Darius to the ship. I will send my carriage to pick up Darius. Once on-board ship, you must become tearful. You must tell him that you have decided you must stay on the island and

await the return of your beloved Arthur. My coachman will ensure that your luggage is not taken aboard. You will then leave
the ship."

"What if Darius leaves as well?"

"Felicity, you must know Darius well enough by now to realise
that his ego will not allow him to pursue you when you have
rejected him for another. He will not want to face his uncle in
light of what we know is their heiress-seeking plan. No, Darius
will sail for England."

"Poor Darius. His uncle will be furious."

"And short of funds when my husband spreads the word of his
financial problems. No one will trust Lord Horace in the city
now. No, my dear, the Plunkett-Browne family will get what
they deserve, and you will be waiting here for your charming
Arthur to return."

"I thought you didn't approve of Arthur."

"I have learnt a great deal recently. I want you to be happy. I
believe that Arthur will be the perfect husband for you."

Felicity looked at her sister and saw she was sincere.

BRIDGWATER

ONCE IT WAS known that the Robert Blake had been sighted
close to the Scilly Isles excitement mounted in the town. Every
day townsfolk gathered at the river side just in case she arrived
earlier than expected. Then it happened. There she was! Pandemonium broke out, there was shouting and cheering, and the
church bells rang out in joy. The crew were safe.

As the ship grew nearer on the incoming tide there was the sudden awareness that there were many more men on board than

expected. People strained their eyes and saw men waving and dancing on the deck. Then one boy, with the eyesight of youth screamed.

"It's Joe, oh my mother! It's brother Joe." Then many familiar faces came into view. The rebels had returned.

There were some who stood silent. Happy for those who were happy, but sad for their own loss.

THE VICARAGE SIX MONTHS LATER

"Such a busy time! Another request for the banns to be read. Tom Turle and Rachael Maidment and Matt Turle and Harriet Ridley are on their second reading.

Our own Anne and John are to have their first reading this coming Sunday and now Thomas Dennis and Mary have come to see me. They will also have their banns read on Sunday."

"Thomas and Mary. I'm so pleased. Hugh....... Mary?

"I am already practicing; the banns will be read as Mary Farai Ganazumba. Mary will be given away by William."

"There is a saying 'marry in haste and repent at leisure' but I support these young people. They have seen so many lose loved ones, they want happiness while they can."

"You are so right Barbara. It's good for Bridgwater; it's good for Somerset. As the young men are returning life is coming back to the county."

"And then there will be christenings......come in." The maid Angela entered.

"Some letters for you vicar. Madam, cook has asked if you could come to the kitchen, she has a new recipe that she would like you to taste." Angela bopped a curtsy and left, followed by Barbara.

A couple of minutes passed, then Barbara returned.

"Cook's come up with a ......Hugh what's wrong." Hugh has a strange expression on his face.

"We have a letter from Arthur."

"At last! It's been so long."

"My dear there is excellent news from our boy, but I fear that you are going to be upset."

"How can I be upset at excellent news?"

"Well, Arthur is now a married man."

"What are you saying?"

"He has married the Honourable Felicity Loveridge in a quiet ceremony in Barbados." There was a gasp from Barbara. Hugh continued reading.

"He begs our forgiveness. He understands that we will be upset that they didn't wait until his contract is finished and they could return home. He knows that you and I will love Felicity when we meet her. He writes that we will be delighted that our son has such a wonderful sweet lady as his wife." Hugh looked up from the letter and saw the shocked expression on his wife's face. She was on her feet; she crossed to Hugh and rudely snatched the letter from him. As she read, her expression darkened.

"I don't believe it! Not to see my only son married. It is my right as a mother, I do not deserve such discourtesy. Oh, I am the most unfortunate of women." Barbara was on the verge of tears.

"Barbara!" Hugh stood and took the letter from his wife. "Whatever has come over you? Of course, you are upset but you are behaving in the most disagreeable manner. Only a few moments ago you said young people have seen so many lose loved ones, they want happiness while they can.

We have all our children living. So many of our neighbours have lost their sons. You should be ashamed of yourself for complaining because you have lost the opportunity to attend your son's wedding. Just be happy that he is happy and pray that we never have to bear the burden of burying our children."

Barbara stared at Hugh, her grey eyes brimming with tears. Hugh used his handkerchief to wipe them away. Slowly her anger melted, then she smiled.

"Oh Hugh, I am so ashamed."

"You should be my girl. Now, come, let us find Anne. She will be delighted to hear her brother's good news.

Folk Ballad of 1692

Oh Lord, where is my husband now
When once he stood beside me?
His body lies at Sedgemoor
In grave of oak and ivy.
Come tell me you who beat the drum,
Why am I so mistreated?
To stand alone, a traitor's wife
My will to live defeated
He swore to me he would be gone
For days but two and twenty
And yet in seven years and more
His bed lies cold and empty

HISTORICAL NOTES

Slave Rebellions

There were three slave rebellions in Barbados in the 1600's, they were all unsuccessful.

The First Slave Rebellion (1649)

Only two plantations were involved. Slaves rebelled because of lack of food. It was rapidly subdued with little damage.

The Second Slave Rebellion (1675)

The rebellion affected the whole island. More than 100 slaves were arrested and tortured, while at least 40 were executed after being found guilty of rebellion. Some committed suicide before being executed, while others were beheaded or burnt alive.

The Third Slave Rebellion (1692)

This also affected the whole island. Over 200 slaves were arrested and over 90 executed after being found guilty of rebellion.

The Battle of Solebay

The battle took place just off the coast of Solebay Suffolk (now called Southwold Bay) on 7th June 1672. It was the first naval battle of the third Anglo-Dutch war. The battle ended inconclusively with both sides claiming victory.

Coach Travel

Coach travel started in England in the 13th century and the coaches were not much better than covered wagons. They were usually drawn by four horses. They had no suspension and could only travel about 5 miles per hour.

The first stagecoach made its appearance in 1610, called by that name because they travelled in segments of 10-15 miles.

Coaching inns started to appear along the roads travelled by the stagecoaches, and some are still standing today. They can be identified by the archways built beside the inn enabling the coach and horses to pass through to the stables at the back of the premises.

Lady Highwayman

The most famous lady highwayman was a noble woman by the name of Katherine Ferrers. She became the sole heir to a considerable fortune at the age of six. A disastrous marriage at the age of 14 resulted in her husband, who had complete control of her assets losing all her money. In an attempt to regain her fortune, she took to robbing stagecoaches. According to legend she also burnt houses, slaughtered livestock and killed a constable. She is believed to have been shot during a robbery.

Vice-Chamberlain of the Household

The Hon. Peregrine Bertie held the office from 1694-1706.

Isolda Parewastel

There is a blue plaque dedicated to Isolda Parewastel in Clare Street (known as Horlokesstrete in the 14th century) in the centre of Bridgwater.

Bridgwater Petition to end slavery

In May 1785, exactly 100 years after Bridgwater men had been transported into slavery Bridgwater was the first town in England to submit a petition calling for the abolition of the Slave Trade.

The petition was presented to Parliament by Bridgwater's two

MPs Messrs Hood and Poulett. It was ordered to 'lie on the table'.... Parliamentary language for 'being politely ignored.'

Acknowledgements

St Matthew's Fair September 1686 - Garry Gillard transcribed the lyrics based on the text from Tide of Change.

Bridgwater Blake Museum https://www.bridgwatermuseum.org.uk

Bridgwater Town Council Website https://bridgwater-tc.gov.uk

Zoylandheritage www.zoylandheritage.co.uk

A History of Bridgwater by John Frederick Lawrence

The Book of Bridgwater by Roger Evans

The internet articles: History of Barbados, History of Slavery, Coronation of William and Mary

Printed in Poland
by Amazon Fulfillment
Poland Sp. z o.o., Wrocław